ENCHANTED

The Duke held her against him, and as her head fell back against his shoulder he looked down at her strange, elfin face.

He ran his finger over her little arched eyebrows, touched her eyes and her small, straight nose. Then he outlined the curve of her lips.

As he did so he felt her quiver with a sensuous movement that was very human, and he laughed gently.

"I am enchanted, my adorable one, not only by your face and your body, but by your spirit, your heart and your soul, and it is an enchantment from which I can never escape."

Bantam Books by Barbara Cartland
Ask your bookseller for the books you have missed

Barbara Cartland's Library of Love Series

THE OBSTACLE RACE

About Barbara Cartland

CRUSADER IN PINK

Enchanted

Barbara Cartland

BANTAM BOOKS
TORONTO • NEW YORK • LONDON • SYDNEY

ENCHANTMENT
A Bantam Book / August 1981

ISBN 0–553–20301–0

Published simultaneously in the United States and Canada

Bantam Books are published by Bantam Books, Inc. Its trade-
mark, consisting of the words "Bantam Books" and the por-
trayal of a bantam, is Registered in U.S. Patent and Trademark
Office and in other countries. Marca Registrada. Bantam
Books, Inc., 666 Fifth Avenue, New York, New York 10103.

Author's Note

Elf once meant all the spirits or demons associated with nature, who were supposed to inhabit the waters, the woods, and the mountains.

To say the word *elf* in all the Germanic languages —and in other languages which have borrowed the word—has a more restricted meaning. The elves were thought of as being handsomer and better made than men, only smaller.

The young female elves would enchant and bewitch a man by their beauty. If he took part in their dancing he was lost and never seen again. Usually their dancing was without witnesses, but in the morning traces of their feet could be seen in the moist grass.

Silvanus, a Latin deity popular in Rome from the very early days, lived in forests and in the mountains and protected agriculture. Several animals were sacred to him—the horse, the wolf and the woodpecker. Among the plants and trees dedicated to his name were the fig tree, the oak, the dogwort and the laurel.

Chapter One

1870

The door of the Library opened and Lady Elfa Allerton immediately lay down on the floor of the balcony.

The Library in the Duke of Northallerton's house was one of its outstanding features, and every visitor exclaimed over its imposing proportions and the intricate brass balcony, which ran round two walls and was reached by a spiral brass staircase.

The bottom part of the balcony-rail was of such a close design of flowers and leaves that when Lady Elfa lay down, it was impossible for her to be seen by anybody in the room below.

Silently pushing her book in front of her, she went on reading, hoping that whoever was below would soon go away.

She suspected that it was her mother, and she knew only too well that if she was seen, she would immediately be sent into the garden on some errand or to work amongst the flowers.

The Duchess of Northallerton was obsessed by her garden, and she could not understand why her children found it boring to cut off dead heads, to plant new acquisitions from various parts of the country or, worse still, to weed the beds.

She had long been convinced that her second daughter Elfa spent far too much time reading, which

1

resulted in her head being in the clouds and her living, as the Duchess often said to whoever would listen, in a dream-world of her own.

Elfa very gently turned over a page and, concentrating on what she was reading, which she found of absorbing interest, she started when she heard her father's voice say sharply:

"So here you are, Elizabeth! I have been looking for you everywhere! I expected you to be in the garden."

"I was looking up how to spell the Latin name for the new azalea which has just arrived," the Duchess replied. "You must come and see it, Arthur! It is a very rare species and I am so excited that it has travelled so well."

"I have something to tell you, Elizabeth," the Duke said, "which is far more exciting than an azalea, or any of the rest of your plants."

"What has happened?" the Duchess asked, a little apprehensively.

She was aware that her stolid, rather prosaic husband was rarely excited about anything, and it was certainly unusual for it to sound in his voice.

"I have settled the question of Magnus Croft once and for all," the Duke said.

"Magnus Croft?" the Duchess repeated.

"Do not be so stupid, Elizabeth! You know as well as I do that I am referring to the 10,000 acres of land which has been a bone of contention between us and Lynchester for the last twenty years."

"Oh—that!" the Duchess exclaimed.

"Yes, that!" the Duke said positively, "and I think nobody except myself could have thought of such an excellent, amicable compromise."

Elfa was listening now because she knew even better than her mother how the dispute over the ownership of Magnus Croft had engendered a feud between two Ducal houses.

While it amused the County, it had resulted in

a bitterness which had prevented the two Dukes from enjoying each other's company.

That the two largest and most important landlords in the neighbourhood should be engaged in a violent squabble had not only been the subject of endless gossip, but it had even resulted in references being made to it in the newspapers.

The latest had infuriated the Duke of Northallerton, who had a contempt for what he termed "the gutter press" and who thought the only justification for the name of any decent Nobleman to appear in print was on the occasions of his birth and of his death.

Because of the enmity in the district known as "the Dukery," Elfa and her sister Caroline had suffered, in that they were not invited to any of the parties which took place in Chester House, the residence of the Duke of Lynchester.

This had not worried them when they were children, for there were a great many other neighbours who were glad to entertain them.

But now that Caroline was grown up and Elfa was to make her début this year, it was infuriating to know that the new Duke, who had inherited two years ago, gave large parties of every sort, from which they were excluded.

"You would not enjoy them anyway!" The Duchess had said positively when they complained to their mother. "The Duke's friends are very much older and more sophisticated than you are and you would feel out of place amongst them."

The way she spoke, in a somewhat repressed manner, told Elfa that her mother disapproved of the Duke's friends.

Yet she could not help thinking they would be more amusing and more interesting than the elderly hunting Squires and County dignitaries who were constantly at Allerton Towers.

Although Caroline had now ceased to be interested in the Duke, Elfa used to see him occasionally in the distance when she was out hunting, and she thought that he looked exactly as a Duke should.

She was therefore listening intently as her mother asked:

"What have you done about the land, Arthur? I am tired of hearing about it and I should have thought the most sensible thing would be for you and the Duke of Lynchester to divide it between you."

"You never listen to anything I say to you, Elizabeth!" her husband roared. "If I have told you once, I have told you over and over again that when the late Duke suggested that to my father, he categorically refused to consider such an idea. He said the land was his and he was damned if he would give it up, even if he was down to his last penny-piece!"

The Duchess sighed.

"I had forgotten that, Arthur."

"Well, you must remember arguments about it. Lynchester always insinuated that my father won it off him at cards when he was too drunk to know what he was doing. All I can say is that if a man gambles when he is in that condition, he deserves all he gets!"

The Duchess sighed again.

She had heard all this dozens of times before. In fact, she could not remember any time during her marriage when the subject of the land that lay between the two Ducal estates had not somehow crept into the conversation.

The whole problem was that the 10,000 acres of Magnus Croft had been some of the best shooting land on the Lynchester Estate, and its woods held more pheasants than any of the Allerton coverts.

She knew, now she thought of it, that the present Duke had started as soon as he inherited to try to persuade her husband to let him buy back the land which had belonged to the Lynchesters for centuries.

The Duke of Northallerton was not particularly short of money, and Magnus Croft was on the extreme edge of his estate and therefore difficult to farm.

But he had no intention of relinquishing what was undoubtedly his by right.

The new Duke of Lynchester was, however, known for his determination.

"I have not told you, simply because you never listen," the Duke went on, "that Lynchester has been at me about this land every time we meet in White's and at every County meeting we both attend. He even approached me on the matter in the hunting-field, which is not a place in which I wish to do business."

"No, of course not," the Duchess said meekly.

"Then today," the Duke went on, "when Lynchester started again after we had discussed the temerity of that new fellow wanting to start another pack of hounds, I had an idea."

"What was it, Arthur?" the Duchess asked, as her husband paused for breath.

As she spoke, she glanced at the sunshine outside and hoped she could soon get back to the garden.

It was an ideal day for bedding out, and she was already late with the plants she had been keeping in the greenhouse until they had grown strong enough to be outside.

"I replied to Lynchester," the Duke said, "'I think these arguments between us have gone on long enough. What I suggest is that we should share the land in a very different way.'

"'What do you mean by that?' he enquired.

"'If you marry my daughter,' I said, "she can have Magnus Croft as part of her dowry.'"

The Duchess gave a little gasp.

"You suggested he should marry Caroline? Arthur, how could you do such a thing?"

"I thought it was extremely astute of me," the Duke answered. "Everybody has been saying that at thirty-four the Duke should be married and produce an heir, and what could be more logical than for Caroline to become his wife?"

"But, Arthur, she is in love with Edward Dalkirk, as you well know."

"The fellow has not a penny to his name!" the Duke retorted, "and Lynchester is undoubtedly the biggest matrimonial catch in the whole country."

"But, Arthur, you promised Caroline that if Edward could make a success with his horses you would permit them to be married."

"I did not promise," the Duke said loftily; "I merely said that I would consider it, and now my answer is no! Caroline will marry Lynchester and the land will be part of the marriage settlement. She will make a very beautiful Duchess and will show the Lynchester diamonds to their advantage."

The Duke's rather hard voice had softened.

He had never disguised the fact that his elder daughter Caroline was his favourite child.

Although he was proud of his two sons, who were at Eton, it was Caroline who filled his heart, if he had one, and she had managed without much difficulty to coax him into saying that she could marry the man she loved.

"But, Arthur!" the Duchess protested. "Caroline is in love!"

"Love! Love!" the Duke said contemptuously. "What has that to do with it? Love comes after marriage, Elizabeth, and Lynchester is not likely to spend very much time with his wife; we all know where his interests lie."

"Really, Arthur, I do not know how you can say such a thing. . . ." the Duchess began.

"Now, Elizabeth, be sensible!" the Duke interrupted. "Lynchester has been pursued by every pretty woman from here to the North Pole ever since he left School but, as you are well aware, all of them, smart, sophisticated and experienced, are married, and he is not likely to cause a scandal by running off with one of them."

"But why Caroline?" the Duchess exclaimed plaintively.

"Must I put it into words of two syllables?" the Duke asked. "Because he wants Magnus Croft, and if he has to marry sooner or later, which he must, what could be more suitable than to take a wife who can bring him a dowry he would really appreciate—10,000 acres of good land which his father lost because he was too drunk to hold his cards straight and which he badly wants and is determined to recover."

"I suppose you realise that Caroline will be broken-hearted?" the Duchess said.

The Duke made a sound that was almost a snort.

"She will get over it," he said sharply. "Young girls always fancy themselves in love with somebody unsuitable, and that is what Edward Dalkirk is, in my opinion."

"You have never thought so until now."

"Whether I did or not is immaterial," the Duke said angrily. "Caroline will marry Lynchester and you will persuade her not to make a fuss, but to obey me in this matter. I have no intention of changing my mind."

"But . . . Arthur . . . !" the Duchess began.

"That is my final word!" the Duke interrupted before she could say any more. "And as Lynchester is coming over tomorrow afternoon, you had better tell her today what to expect."

"But . . . Arthur . . . . !" the Duchess began again.

There was the sound of the Library door shutting sharply and the Duke was gone.

Elfa did not move. She had lain rigid on the floor of the balcony ever since her father had begun to speak.

She felt as if she had been holding her breath the whole time; only when she heard her mother also leave the room did she gasp for air.

Could it be possible that her father had arranged anything so cruel, so utterly diabolical?

7

She knew that if she had not heard what had been said with her own ears, she would never have believed it.

Stiffly she rose to her feet, put the book she had been reading back on the shelf and hurried down the twisting brass steps to the floor.

Then she started to run as swiftly as she could, out of the Library, down a long passage which led, not to the magnificent front Hall with its marble floor and statues, but to a side staircase.

This led to the second floor, where the two girls slept and where what had been their School-Room had now, with the departure of Elfa's Governess, been converted into their own special Sitting-Room.

Elfa was breathless by the time she reached the door, and she paused for a moment, not only to get back her breath but also to collect her thoughts.

How could she tell Caroline? What could she say?

She knew as she opened the door that she was like the messenger of Doom in a Greek tragedy.

* * *

"I . . . cannot! I cannot . . . lose . . . Edward!" Caroline said for the hundredth time.

Even while tears were running down her face, her sister thought she still looked lovely and that no man, not even the Duke of Lynchester, for all his smart, sophisticated women, could fail to find her attractive.

"I know, dearest," Elfa said, "but Papa is determined, and I cannot think for the moment what we can do to prevent the Duke from offering for you."

"I . . . can . . . say no," Caroline said in a tremulous voice.

"I do not think he would listen, nor would Papa, now that he has made up his mind."

Elfa had tried to break the news as gently as she could to Caroline.

At first her sister had grown so pale that she

thought she might faint; then she burst into floods of tears.

Caroline was not a strong character. She was sweet, gentle, very amenable, and so lovely that every man who looked at her looked again.

She was actually, Elfa thought secretly, exactly the type that the Duke would envisage as his ideal Duchess. She was tall, nearly five feet and nine inches. She had fair hair, the colour of ripening corn, blue eyes and a pink-and-white complexion.

She had never in her whole life caused her parents a moment's anxiety until she fell in love with Edward Dalkirk.

She was so much in love with him that no other man existed for her. Any who had wished to court her had found it impossible to hold her attention or even to make her aware of their existence; any ideas they had of wooing her soon vanished.

The Duke had nothing against Edward except that he was poor.

He was the only son of Viscount Dalkirk, who had a crumbling Castle on an impoverished estate in Scotland, and when Edward left his Regiment, in which he had served with distinction, he had decided to try to make a little money by breeding horses.

This ambition was facilitated by the fact that his uncle had left him a house and 500 acres on the borders of the Duke of Northallerton's land, which was how he had met Caroline.

From that moment, because he loved her as deeply as she loved him, he had worked feverishly to make enough money so that he could ask her to be his wife.

Unfortunately, breeding the right type of horses from the quality of mares he could afford to buy took time, and he had not anticipated that he would be able to approach the Duke for at least another year.

"I suppose you could run away together," Elfa said,

"and hide somewhere where Papa would not find you."

"In which . . . case Edward would lose the . . . money he has . . . invested in his horses, and we could not afford to find another house to live in. But I cannot marry the . . . Duke! I must marry Edward!" Caroline wailed. "I love him! I love . . . him . . . and I would . . . die if I had to marry any . . . other man!"

Elfa rose to her feet and walked to the window.

She was very fond of her sister, and it hurt her to see her so unhappy.

But while she turned over and over in her mind every argument by which Caroline could try to persuade her father that she must marry Edward Dalkirk, Elfa was quite certain the Duke would not listen to her.

She had always known he was ambitious for Caroline.

He had been proud when she was acclaimed a beauty, and looking back, Elfa could remember the expression of personal triumph on his face when Caroline had looked so lovely at her first Ball.

It had been two years ago. Elfa herself had been a school-girl at the time, but she had thought then, with a little twist of her lips, that when it was her turn to have a Ball, her father would not be proud of her in the same way.

She could understand that the Duke, who had always wanted the child he loved best to shine, would glory in the fact that Caroline could wear a coronet of strawberry leaves, and that her social position, after the Royal Family, would be undoubtedly the most important in England.

Elfa knew that there had always been a rivalry in rank and importance between the two Ducal houses whose lands marched side by side.

The old Duke of Lynchester had been a somewhat dissolute character, and so her father had been much more respected and admired in the County, which consequently had become, to all intents and purposes, his Empire.

But the new Duke, who had recently inherited, was different.

He was a friend of the Prince of Wales and, as far as Elfa could gather, the leader of the Social Set in London, which was acclaimed and envied by those who were not shocked by it. And he undoubtedly had an influence that had something imperial about it.

As she thought of the Duke, this was not surprising.

In the hunting field he stood out, not only as a superlative rider to hounds, but also as a personality it was impossible to ignore.

She had never spoken to him, but she was quite certain that she would find him overbearing and even intimidating, and she knew a man such as this would leave Caroline crushed and helpless.

Because Caroline had always been so amenable, it was Elfa, even though she was two years younger, who had been the leader, the instigator of all their pranks, and who, if they were punished, protected Caroline by taking the blame herself.

In a way this was only fair, because Caroline had little imagination and it was Elfa who, as her father often pointed out, had too much.

"What can I . . . do? What . . . can I do?" Caroline murmured now, and she went on crying into a handkerchief that was already soaked with her tears. "I cannot marry the Duke!"

Even when she was crying she still looked very lovely, although her nose was now slightly pink and her blue eyes were swimming with tears.

"There must be something," Elfa said, almost beneath her breath.

Then she gave a sudden cry.

"I have an idea!"

11

Caroline did not reply. She just seemed to sink a little lower in her chair and her hands went up once again to her eyes.

Elfa was standing very still.

"It is coming to me," she said. "I can see it like a picture unfolding in front of my eyes. I can do it! I know I can do it!"

"Do ... what?" Caroline asked dully.

"Save you!" Elfa answered.

"From ... marrying the Duke?"

"Yes, from marrying the Duke," Elfa repeated.

"How? How?" Caroline asked. "I know Papa will not ... listen to me, and Edward has ... no money at the ... moment. He told me when I saw him ... yesterday that he had to borrow from the Bank to buy those last mares."

"If Edward borrowed a million pounds," Elfa said, "it would still not save you from being a Duchess."

"I know ... I know, but I do not ... want to be a Duchess! I just want to marry Edward and live in that ... dear little house ... alone with him."

Caroline's voice was almost incoherent, and now the tears were running down her cheeks and spilling onto the front of her gown.

"Listen," Elfa said. "Listen to me, Caroline."

She went down on her knees in front of her sister and took her hands in hers.

"I have thought of how I can save you," she said, "but you have to do, dearest, exactly what I tell you—you promise?"

"I will promise ... anything if it means I can ... marry Edward."

"Very well," Elfa said. "Now listen to me ...."

*   *   *

The Duke of Lynchester watched the Duke of Northallerton's carriage drive away from his front door. Then he walked across the Hall and into the Study, where he habitually sat.

12

It was a comfortable, well-designed room, and although there were a few books, the walls were mostly covered with a magnificent collection of paintings of horses, which he had transferred from various other rooms in the house.

The artists were mainly Stubbs, Sartorious and Herring and had been collected by one of his ancestors. By rehanging them together, the Duke knew he had improved one room in the house out of all recognition, and he was determined gradually to bring the others to the same state of perfection.

He was, although he did not admit it to himself, a perfectionist, and he liked everything around him to please both his eye and his mind.

It had always annoyed him that Chester House had been left in what he thought was a state of disarrangement by his father and doubtless his grandfather before him.

It was an exceedingly impressive building, having been completed in about 1750, and at the time it was a model both of Georgian architecture and of Georgian taste, acclaimed by everybody who saw it.

The Second Duke had been concerned only with women and horses, and the third had an obsession for gambling, which had cost the estate a great deal of money and the loss of a number of important paintings.

The gaps caused by their sale had been filled in haphazardly with any paintings of about the same size which could be transferred from a less important part of the house. The result was, the present Duke decided, neither artistic nor pleasing.

However, he was now getting the house as he wanted it and, although the house had certainly acquired a new grace and artistry, he knew, when he thought about it, that what it lacked was a woman's touch.

This, unfortunately, could be imparted only when he had a wife to share the great building with him.

13

For years he had been determined not to marry, knowing it would interfere with the very amusing life he lived in London and the pleasure he derived from not one woman but a number of women.

Now, however, without the prompting of his relatives, he was well aware that it was time for producing children, especially an heir to carry on the succession.

"If you wait much longer you will be too old to teach your son how to become a game-shot and how to ride," his grandmother had said tartly when last he saw her.

He had not replied, and she added:

"It distresses me to think of the Lynchester diamonds shut away in a safe, the pearls doubtless losing their lustre and growing green because they are not worn against a warm skin."

The Duke had laughed, but he was aware that his grandmother was talking sense.

But when he had thought about it later, he had wondered how one set about getting married when in the Social World, in which he reigned as a King in his own right, he seldom, if ever, encountered a young girl.

There were of course numbers of them there for the asking, standing beside their Chaperons, and looking, he thought, dull, gauche, and quite beneath his condescension.

At the house-parties that he gave himself and at those he attended, the guests were chosen with particular care and with one primary consideration: that they should be entertaining. This, as far as the Duke was concerned, implied two other qualities—they must be alluring and bewitching!

That was certainly what he had found in the sophisticated beauties who looked at him knowingly from under their long eyelashes, pouted their red lips provocatively, and made it very clear that they were as willing as he was for a fiery *affaire de coeur*.

These, the Duke knew, had all the thrill of a sound day's hunting—a run for his money, the joy of the chase, and the satisfaction of the kill. It was most enjoyable and in theory no one was hurt.

This in fact was an assumption which did not always prove true.

The women with whom the Duke engaged himself had a way, when he made love to them, of not only losing their heads but also their hearts.

He often wondered, when he was feeling introspective, why it was that, once a woman came to love him passionately, possessively and demandingly, after far too short a time he himself invariably became bored and restless.

He wondered why he suddenly ceased to desire them and began to look for a new face, a new interest.

He came to the conclusion that it was because when he was not making love to them he began to anticipate exactly what they would say and do, the allurements they would use, the enticements that he had met before.

Then all he wanted was to close the door on what had been a short, fiery encounter and forget about it.

But in practice it was not as easy as that—and women who were in love with him clung, complained and reproached him.

That was what he found boring in the extreme, and he sometimes asked himself if it was really worthwhile.

He liked women, he thought, as much as he liked horses, and he could not imagine life without either of them. He would like also to have children.

Just recently he had been thinking that he would teach his son, when he had one, to appreciate the improvements he had made on Chester House.

He would show him how to hunt with the pack of fox-hounds of which he was Master, and he would

15

certainly start him shooting at an early age, so that he
would become as outstanding a game-shot as he was
himself.

He would also teach him to fish the trout in the
lake. Then he would take him to Scotland, where he
would never forget the excitement of catching his first
salmon when he was twelve years of age.

The Duke of Northallerton's proposition that he
should marry his daughter Caroline had in a way
come like a bomb-shell. At the same time the Duke,
when he thought it over, decided it could be a satis-
factory solution to the problem that had been perturb-
ing his mind for some time.

He remembered being told that Lady Caroline Allerton was a great beauty, and he thought, although he
was not sure, that he had noticed her in the hunting
field.

Tall, fair and blue-eyed, she would certainly look
her best wearing the sapphires which had been his
mother's favourite set of jewels, and he was sure she
would grace the turquoises, which would doubtless
match her eyes.

What was more important than anything else was
that the land called Magnus Croft would come back
into the possession of the Lynchester Estate.

It had always infuriated the Duke that his father
should have parted so foolishly with any of their land.

He had only to look at the map which hung in the
Estate Office to feel a surge of anger, when he saw
how the Magnus Croft acres, which dipped right into
the estate in the shape of a teapot spout, were coloured
green instead of red, which depicted all the rest of his
land.

"Now I am getting things exactly as they should
be," the Duke told himself.

He wondered what Isobel would think when she
heard he was to be married.

The Countess of Walshingham was his current mistress and he was not yet bored with her.

16

She was far more witty than the other women with whom he had been involved during the past years. She made him laugh, which was unusual, even though he was aware that everything she said was at somebody else's expense.

But the mere fact that she looked so lovely when she was being her most spiteful and her blue eyes were glinting with venom really added to her charms.

He found too that her fiery response to his lovemaking was more intense and indeed more demanding than anything he had known for some time.

He knew he had no wish for the moment to give up the Countess or resist her appeal.

Moreover, he told himself, there was no reason why marriage should interfere with his other interests, as long as they were discreetly conducted.

He had every intention of treating his wife with respect and doing nothing to embarrass her or even to make her aware that he was unfaithful.

As his wife and a Duchess, she was entitled to her place by his side, and he knew that, whether they were at Buckingham Palace, Windsor Castle or Chester House, he would see that she was received and treated as befitted her position.

"She shall have no regrets on that score," the Duke decided.

The only difference, therefore, in his behaviour in the future from what it had been in the past would be that his meetings with Isobel or any other woman who took his fancy would have to be far more discreet.

He would have to be clever to deceive the sharp-eyed gossips who were always ready to make trouble, but he was sure he could outwit them.

The Duke sat down at his desk to inspect the pile of letters and invitations that his secretary had put there for his perusal.

As he did so, the door opened.

The Duke looked up with a smile.

"Hello, Harry! I am delighted to see you! I am glad you have arrived early before the rest of the party."

He rose as he spoke and held out his hand, and Harry Sheldon, who was one of his oldest friends, replied:

"I was intending to break your record getting here, but I have to concede my horses are not as good as yours."

"How long did you take?"

"Two hours, twenty-three minutes."

"Ten minutes too slow."

"I know that," Harry Sheldon replied; "there is no need to rub it in."

He threw himself down in an armchair, saying as he did so:

"All the same I deserve a glass of champagne, and I hope it is cool enough to drink."

"You insult my household arrangements," the Duke replied.

He walked towards the table in the corner of the room, where there was an open bottle of champagne in a gold ice-cooler.

"You missed a good party last night, Silvanus," Harry Sheldon said. "We dined at White's and went on to a new House of Pleasure that has just opened in the Haymarket. There were some little lovebirds from France that are the prettiest things you have ever seen. All 'Oooh-la-la' and a lot of *'Oui—Oui!'* I enjoyed myself."

"You can take me there next week," the Duke said as he walked across the room with a glass of champagne in his hand. "And by the way, Harry, I am going to be married!"

Harry Sheldon almost dropped the glass of champagne his friend had just given him.

"Did you say—married?"

The Duke nodded.

"Good God!" Harry exclaimed. "So you have taken

the plunge at last! But who the devil to? And why have I not met her?"

"I have not met her myself, for that matter," the Duke answered.

"Are you serious?"

"Completely!"

"Then what are you saying, and who is she?"

"She is the Duke of Northallerton's daughter. He has just offered her to me, together with the 10,000 acres of Magnus Croft."

"I do not believe it!"

"It is true."

"Then you have won!" Harry Sheldon said. "You swore you would get back that land your father threw away on the turn of a card."

"Yes, I have won, and I believe it is tied up with a rather pretty ribbon. I have been told that Caroline Allerton is a beauty."

"Caroline Allerton? But you have never met her?"

"Of course not. The Lynchesters have not been on calling terms with the Northallertons since the Duke refused to hand back the land when my father explained that, owing to the influence of alcohol, he was not in his right senses when he staked and lost it."

"Who can blame him?" Harry Sheldon remarked. "A bet is a bet, and a point of honour."

"Exactly!" the Duke said. "At the same time, my father thought the Duke was unreasonable and cut off communications except on a strictly official basis."

"And was it on a strictly official basis that you were offered his daughter?"

"Very strictly," the Duke replied. "We have a common enemy in the fact that an outsider is attempting to introduce a new pack of fox-hounds into the County. There are two packs already, one of which I own, the other in which the Duke of Northallerton has an interest, so you see we had to combine to put the bounder back in the kennels from which he emerged."

19

"And the end result of this peculiar partnership is that you decided to marry the Duke's daughter."

"He suggested it," the Duke said, "and as it seemed to me a sensible arrangement, I agreed."

Harry threw back his head and laughed.

"Sensible!" he exclaimed when he could speak. "My dear Silvanus, how can it be sensible to marry a girl you have never seen just because she can bring you some land which, like Naboth's Vineyard, you have always coveted?"

"And justifiably, since the Vineyard in question has always belonged to the Lynchester Estate," the Duke said loftily.

"Damn it all, think of taking a wife on such terms!"

"Why not? She is well-bred—nobody can dispute that—I am told she is a beauty, and quite frankly, Harry, I think it is time I married."

"I have thought that for the last five years!" his friend said. "It is time you settled down, and most of all you need an heir."

"You might be my grandmother speaking."

"Your grandmother has a lot of sense, but as an old friend I must warn you that this is not the right way to go about marriage."

"You speak as an authority, of course!" the Duke said mockingly.

"No, but I can tell you one thing: I shall never tie myself to a woman unless I am quite certain I am fond of her and that I can stand her conversation at breakfast."

"There is no law to say you have to breakfast with your wife," the Duke protested.

"There is no law that says you have to listen to her," Harry replied, "but it is something which is inevitable when marriage is concerned."

The Duke stood with his back to the fireplace, and there was an expression on his face which told his friend he was being obstinate.

"It is all very well, Harry," he said, "to carp and find fault, but you and Grandmama are united with a dozen of my other relatives in saying that I should be married!"

"As you should," Harry murmured.

"But I am not a callow boy who is likely to fall in love with a pretty face," the Duke went on, "and I am not so half-baked as to think that a girl straight out of the school-room is likely to be amusing or know anything about the subjects which interest me."

Harry started to speak but the Duke put out his hand to stop him.

"Let me finish," he said. "I have thought this out carefully. As I have no wish to have a wife who is promiscuous, I am obliged to marry somebody young. I shall hope that she is intelligent enough to make herself pleasant not only to me, but to my friends, and if she has been well brought up she will grace the end of my table and learn with few mistakes to be a good hostess."

"I accept all that," Harry said, "but what about when you are alone together?"

There was a faint smile on the Duke's face as he replied:

"There, I admit, you have a point. But why should we be alone except on very rare occasions?"

He walked across the room before he went on:

"In the old days, as you are well aware, in a house of this size there lived not only the Duke and the Duchess—or, before my great-grandfather received the title, the Marquis and Marchioness of Chester!"

He smiled slightly as he continued:

"There were their children, other relatives, grandmothers, great-aunts, cousins, old friends, a Chaplain, Nurses, Governesses, Tutors of every sort! In fact, the house was permanently filled with people, apart from the guests who, one learns from the diaries of the time, were entertained with lavish hospitality all through the year."

Harry laughed.

"So that is the sort of life you are planning, that of a *pater familias*, or should I say a King in a Court of his own? I hope I shall be invited to be the Court Jester."

"Could you be anything else?" the Duke asked. "But seriously, Harry, you see the idea?"

"Of course I see it, and I hope your cardboard Duchess is exactly what you expect her to be, a puppet on strings that you pull, and that when you pull them she will dance until you walk away and ignore her."

"Stop preaching at me," the Duke ordered. "You know as well as I do that this has been a traditional way of living since the age of Elizabeth, when the first Chester built a house here and invited the Queen to stay."

"Did she come?"

"Of course, and he spent an exorbitant amount of money in entertaining her."

"Well, you cannot invite the Queen, for who would want the Widow of Windsor?" Harry said. "But the Prince of Wales will undoubtedly enjoy your parties, and so of course will—Isobel."

There was something in the way which Harry referred to the Countess which made the Duke know he was asking a question.

"Yes, and so will Isobel," he repeated slowly, looking his friend straight in the eyes.

"Then I can only hope for her sake that your Duchess is half-witted," Harry said. "Otherwise she will be seared by Isobel's tongue, tortured by her innuendos, and undoubtedly, unless you prevent it, reduced to tears within five minutes of Isobel's entering the house."

"I can control Isobel," the Duke replied, "and I shall not allow her to do anything of the sort."

"I wonder if you will be able to prevent her," Harry said. "She will be like a lioness defending her mate against all comers, and your wife will hardly have a fair chance when it comes to a fight with claws."

"It will not come to that," the Duke said sharply, "and anyway, I will see that everybody, including you, treats my wife with respect."

"I have always thought that the word *respect*, together with *duty*, *obligation* and *responsibility*, is of unutterable dullness," Harry said. "If your wife has any spirit in her, she will want a great deal more than respect."

"Shut up, Harry!" the Duke ordered. "You are trying to make me regret that I accepted the Duke of Northallerton's offer, and tomorrow I am going to the Towers to ask his daughter formally for her hand in marriage."

Harry Sheldon did not answer, and after a moment the Duke said:

"Dammit, what is the alternative? You want me to marry. I have been nagged about it for years, and now you are trying to put obstacles in my way. If I do not marry Caroline Allerton, it will be some other unfledged school-girl."

There was silence for a moment. Then Harry said:

"But of course nobody else can offer you so much land."

"Nobody! And whatever happens, future generations of Chesters will undoubtedly bless me for the sacrifice I am making on their behalf."

"Sacrifice? That is the right word!" Harry said. "Or shall I say you are selling your freedom for a 'mess of pottage'?"

"For 10,000 acres," the Duke said laconically.

"I have a feeling," Harry said prophetically, "that you will pay one way or another for every acre, one by one."

The Duke laughed.

"If I have any more of your gloomy predictions I shall send you back to London," he said. "What you

23

need is another glass of champagne! Oh, and I forgot
to tell you—amongst my other guests there will be the
delectable Marguerite, who is arriving this evening
especially for you."

Harry Sheldon sat up and there was a sudden light
in his eyes.

"She has accepted?"

"With alacrity!" the Duke replied, "and—hold your
breath—she is coming alone. James is unfortunately
detained on duty at Buckingham Palace."

Harry Sheldon made a sound of undisguised exalta-
tion.

"Silvanus, you are a Trojan! You have brought a
new light and laughter into my life, and one day I
shall do the same for you."

"I will hold you to that!" the Duke said. "God
knows, if I am to become a married man, I may need
your help."

Chapter Two

"You are very quiet!" the Duke complained accusingly.

He was speaking to everybody seated at the dining-room table, but he was looking at Caroline.

Elfa also looked at her apprehensively. She was aware that Caroline was controlling her feelings with the utmost difficulty.

She had been prepared when, earlier in the morning, her father had sent for her and said:

"I have some very good news for you, Caroline. In fact, I consider you are a very lucky girl."

"Why, Papa?"

"Because the Duke of Lynchester wishes to marry you, and is calling this afternoon to ask you formally to be his wife."

If the Duke was apprehensive about what his daughter's reaction would be, he did not show it, except that perhaps his voice was louder and he spoke a little more positively than usual.

Although that was what she knew her father was going to say, Caroline nearly burst into tears.

Then she recalled Elfa's strict instructions and managed to say:

"It is a ... big surprise ..., Papa, but a ... great honour."

"That is what I knew you would think," the Duke said with satisfaction. "It is a very great honour, and I can imagine nothing more pleasing, my dear, than to see you a Duchess and know you are living next door."

Caroline had escaped from him as soon as she could and run up the stairs to the School-Room, to fling her arms around Elfa.

She was trembling and it was impossible for her to speak.

"Did you answer as I told you to?" Elfa asked.

Caroline nodded.

"That was sensible of you," Elfa said. "He must not suspect for a moment that you intend to oppose him."

"But suppose...just suppose..." Caroline began in a frightened voice.

"Leave everything to me," Elfa interrupted. "Just be quiet and composed at luncheon and say as little as possible."

"I shall cry...I know...I shall...cry," Caroline murmured.

"If you do, you will ruin everything," Elfa said. "This is our only chance, Caroline, and if you mess it up then there will be nothing I or anybody else can do to save you from marrying the Duke."

This threat made her try frantically to do as Elfa told her.

Now, before Caroline could reply to her father, Elfa said quickly:

"I think it is the weather which is giving Caroline a headache."

"Who says she has a headache?" the Duke enquired, turning his attention to his younger daughter.

"She said she had one when she woke up," Elfa replied, "and that made me think there might be thunder in the air."

"Fiddlesticks!" the Duke said sharply.

He looked down the table at his wife.

"If Caroline has a headache, see she has something .o cure it," he said, "and that she is dressed in her prettiest gown by three o'clock."

"Three o'clock?" the Duchess questioned, thinking this would shorten drastically her time in the garden.

"Lynchester should be calling about an h ur later," the Duke explained, "but I do not want you all scurrying about like a lot of scraggy hens because you are not ready."

"No, of course not, Arthur," the Duchess agreed.

"So I expect you and Caroline to be in the Drawing-Room at three o'clock."

"Very well, Arthur."

The Duke then went into a long monologue about the iniquities of people who came into a County and thought they could run it.

The Duchess was not listening, nor was Caroline, but Elfa knew her father was still resentful of the unfortunate gentleman who was trying to have his own pack of fox-hounds.

Because she wished to keep his attention from Caroline, she asked some intelligent questions, which the Duke answered either angrily or contemptuously, but she managed to make the subject last out the meal.

Then, as the Duchess hurried away for a few minutes in the garden before she would have to change her gown, Caroline and Elfa went upstairs.

"I really . . . have got a . . . headache," Caroline complained.

"Of course you have," Elfa replied sympathetically, "and you have to convince Mama when she comes upstairs to fetch you that you are too ill to move."

"What if she . . . drags me . . . downstairs?" Caroline asked in a frightened whisper.

"She will hardly do that if you are wearing, as I told you, nothing but your bodice and your petticoats. You throw your gown over a chair as if you were just about to step into it, then you are overcome and collapse on the bed."

"Oh, Elfa . . . I am . . . frightened! Suppose . . . she does not . . . believe me?"

27

"Think of Edward and you will be able to act very convincingly," Elfa answered. "The one thing we have to do is to prevent the Duke seeing how pretty you are."

Caroline sat down limply on a chair and Elfa went to her own room to change into her riding-clothes.

At half-past-two, having given Caroline some last-minute instructions, Elfa went down the stairs and out by a side-door to find her way to the stables.

The Head Groom looked at her in surprise.

"Oi wasn't expectin' ye this afternoon, M'Lady!" he said, with the familiarity of an old servant. "Oi thought 'e would be too busy up at t'house seein' His Grace."

Elfa was not in the least surprised that Garston knew that the Duke of Lynchester was coming to call, and the reason for it.

As her father always talked at meals as if the servants were deaf or without any human curiosity, she knew that by this time everybody in the house would know that the feud between the two Dukes had ended, and the reason why.

"I am not wanted," she said to Garston, "and as you know, Swallow needs exercise."

Swallow was her own special horse, and Garston was smiling as he said:

"That's true enough, M'Lady, but ye'll have to tak Duster wi' ye to keep up wi' 'im."

"Duster will do very well," Elfa replied, "and Ben can ride him."

"Ben?" Garston questioned. "Your Ladyship alles rides wi' Jim."

"I want Ben this afternoon," Elfa insisted.

Ben was the most unintelligent of the stable-boys and could always be relied upon to do exactly as he was told without question.

Five minutes later Elfa was riding Swallow across the Park.

The horse was fresh, skittish and difficult to handle while he was being saddled, but because Elfa was on his back he responded, as he always did, to her slightest touch.

She soon forgot everything but the joy of being carried more swiftly than the wind on a superlative animal whom she loved more than anyone or anything else in the world.

She rode across the Park and over the fields. Then she headed northeast across country, a direction in which she seldom rode.

She knew that if Jim had been with her, he would have been asking curious questions as to where they were going, but Ben just plodded along behind, concentrating on keeping Duster up with Swallow.

They rode to where a dusty lane cut through the Allerton estate and joined the land belonging to the Duke of Lynchester.

Here Elfa drew Swallow in, aware that from the particular vantage point at which she had stopped, she could see for a long way, and that a high Phaeton would be visible for at least a mile before it reached her.

Ben had brought Duster up behind her but said nothing, only sitting stolidly and comfortably in the saddle.

There was nothing in sight and Elfa turned round.

"Listen, Ben," she said, "we have come here because, as I expect you know, the Duke of Lynchester is calling this afternoon at the house."

"Oi hears tha,' M'Lady," Ben replied.

"Lady Caroline and my Mother wished to be ready to receive His Grace when he arrives, but as you are well aware, Her Grace will not want to leave the garden until the last moment."

"No, M'Lady."

"What I want you to do," Elfa continued, "the moment we glimpse His Grace approaching, is to ride

29

back as fast as you can to let Emily, who will be
waiting at the Servants' Hall entrance, know that His
Grace is on his way."

"Emily, M'Lady?" Ben questioned.

"Yes, Emily," Elfa replied.

Emily was the youngest housemaid of those who
looked after her and Caroline, and Elfa had given her
instructions to be waiting at the kitchen door at five
minutes to three.

"As soon as Emily gets my message," she had said
to Caroline, "take off your gown and lie on your bed
with the blinds half-drawn. Put a handkerchief
dipped in eau de Cologne on your forehead, and
when Mama comes upstairs, speak every word slowly,
as if you are finding it difficult to enunciate."

"I shall . . . never be . . . able to do it . . . convincingly," Caroline had answered, but Elfa had not listened.

Now, to make sure that Ben had understood his
instructions, she repeated them again.

"When you have given Emily the message," she
went on, "ride back the way we came here. Then, in
case I have taken a different direction, stop at the
edge of the Park and wait for me there."

She saw Ben looked a little bewildered, and she
said it again and hoped he would understand.

"We must ride home together," she finished. "You
know His Grace does not like my riding without a
groom."

She thought this last remark would ensure that Ben
would not linger to gossip with the servants at the
back-door, or go to the stable-yard and tell them what
had occurred.

The one safeguard against this happening was that
Ben was not a talker, while Jim was.

As Elfa thought it was a mistake to distract Ben's
mind from what he had to do, she continued to look at
the road over the Lynchester estate.

Then, when Swallow was beginning to fidget, she
saw in the far distance a movement.

There was no mistaking that it was in fact a Phaeton, being driven by a gentleman wearing a tall hat, or that the pair of horses drawing it were travelling swiftly. Elfa turned her head.

"The Phaeton is coming! Go back as quickly as you can, Ben, and do not waste a minute!"

Obediently Ben turned Duster round, and as he set off at a gallop, Elfa rode in the opposite direction alongside the lane.

About a mile on, there was a wood and Elfa rode Swallow slowly out of the field and into the centre of the dusty road.

Again she sat waiting, aware that her heart was beating uncomfortably in her breast, and her lips felt dry.

Suppose she failed? Suppose after all her plans the Duke would not listen to her? Then Caroline's heart would be broken and, whatever the consequences, she and Edward would have to run away together.

Because she was nervous, it seemed to Elfa that she had been waiting an unconscionable time, and she began to be afraid that the Duke might have changed his mind and turned back.

Then, as she saw the Phaeton coming down the road towards her, she realised that the horses which His Grace was driving were better than any animal her father owned, and the Phaeton itself was a smart, new model which had not been seen in the County until now.

At first when he saw a woman in the centre of the road in front of him the Duke did not pull in his horses.

He expected her to move to one side to let him pass, and only when he realised she had no intention of doing so did he bring his team to a standstill.

She still did not move. Then, as he waited, she rode over the grass to the side of his Phaeton.

"Good afternoon, Your Grace!"

The Duke raised his hat.

31

"Good afternoon! I do not think we have met."

"No, but I wish to speak to Your Grace on a very important matter."

The Duke raised his eyebrows before he replied:

"I am in fact in somewhat of a hurry. Could we not make an appointment to meet at a more convenient time?"

"This time is convenient for me, Your Grace, and the matter I have to discuss with you is not only of great importance, but most urgent!"

"Then I am prepared to listen to what you have to say."

"Thank you," Elfa replied, "but as it is confidential, I hope it would not be asking too much of Your Grace if you would walk with me into the shelter of the wood."

Now the Duke looked at her in astonishment, and Elfa thought for one terrifying moment that he was about to refuse.

Then, as if he were slightly amused, he said:

"Very well, but I hope this is not some joke, or that I shall be sprung on by Highwaymen and held to ransom for the meagre amount I carry in my pocket."

"I can promise Your Grace faithfully that none of those things will happen," Elfa said.

"Very well."

The Duke turned his head, but there was no need to give the order to his groom, who was perched in the seat behind, to go to his horses' heads, and by the time the Duke had fixed the reins on the buckboard in front of him, his horses were being held.

He stepped lightly down to the ground and saw that Elfa had already dismounted.

"What about your horse?" he enquired.

"Swallow will follow me," Elfa replied.

She walked ahead of the Duke round to the back of the Phaeton and into the field at the side of the wood.

A few steps took them under the trees, and she saw, as she had expected, because she knew the wood well, that at the edge of it, waiting for collection from the road, were a number of tree-trunks.

She sat down on one of them and the Duke, somewhat gingerly, did the same.

"Now," he said. "What is all this about? An' suppose we start by your introducing yourself. I ga'her you know who I am!"

"Yes, Your Grace, and my na ne is Mary Margaret Alexandra Elfa Allerton."

The Duke's lips twitched, but before he could speak, Elfa added:

"But I am always called 'Elfa' for very obvious reasons."

The Duke looked at her and was definitely amused. He had thought when she first spoke to him that she looked unusual and quite unlike any young woman he had ever seen before.

Now he knew it was because there was something definitely elfin about her, though he might not have recognised that fact if she had not told him her name.

Her eyes, which were very large in her small, pointed face, slanted upwards at the corners, and there was something about her, the Duke thought, that he connected in his mind with the illustrations of the fairy-tales he had read when he was in the Nursery.

Strangely enough, her mouth was the same, a very pretty mouth, and yet at the corners it definitely had an upwards slant. When she smiled there were two dimples, quite deep ones, in her cheeks.

She looked up at the Duke.

"When I was born," she explained, as if he had asked the question, "Papa was quite certain I was a Changeling, and because everybody said I looked like a small elf, my Godmother, who had a sense of humour, added the name Elfa as she handed me to the Clergyman at the font. Papa was furious about it, but there was nothing he could do."

"I can only say that it is very appropriate," the Duke remarked.

Elfa smiled at him and pulled off her riding-hat.

"It is more comfortable without a hat, and I only wore it to impress you."

"You thought that was necessary?"

He asked the question automatically because again he was thinking that her hair, like her face, was different.

It should have been the colour of beech-leaves, but it was so splashed with gold, as if by sunshine, that instead it seemed to glow almost like a light against the green of the trees.

Without a hat Elfa certainly appeared even more elfin than human, and she was so slender that it was difficult to think of her as a woman. Her fingers, from which she now drew her riding-gloves, were long and slim and, the Duke noticed, very white.

"Well, Lady Elfa," he said aloud, "now that we have established our identities, will you tell me this important secret that you wish to impart?"

Sitting very still with her hands in her lap, Elfa looked at the Duke, and he saw that just as her hair glowed with what seemed a strange light, so did her eyes.

At the same time he had the feeling she was looking at him as if she were appraising him, searching deep beneath the surface, but for what he had no idea.

Actually, apart from being afraid about what she had to say, Elfa was thinking that the Duke was even better looking than he had appeared in the distance.

At the same time she was aware that there was something authoritative and perhaps frightening about him.

She had expected him to have an air of consequence, but not to seem quite so overwhelmingly omnipotent, if that was the right word.

He was magnificent and at the same time positively majestic, and she thought he would also be exceedingly determined and perhaps obstinate.

"Well, what have you to say?" the Duke asked, and now there was a note of impatience in his tone.

"Quite simply, Your Grace," Elfa said, "I am well aware that you are on your way to ask my sister to marry you. But instead, would you be so obliging as to marry me?"

If she had intended to surprise the Duke, Elfa realised that she had succeeded.

He did not move or start, but she saw an incredulous expression come into his eyes. Then his lips set in a hard line.

"Is this a joke?" he demanded.

"Certainly not," Elfa answered. "It is a very serious request, and also a plea for help."

"What do you mean by that?"

"My sister Caroline, who my father wishes should marry you, is deeply in love with somebody else. They had hoped to be married in a year's time, but now my father has told Caroline she has to be a Duchess. If she is forced to do so, it will break her heart."

The Duke looked as if he felt that what he was hearing could not be true, and it struck Elfa that in making the arrangements with her father, the Duke had never for one moment contemplated the fact that Caroline would not be delighted at the idea of marrying him.

She supposed that, after having been pursued by so many women who, if her father was to be believed, found him irresistibly alluring, it was a shock for the Duke to find that there was one girl, at any rate, who had no wish to be his wife.

The Duke did not speak, and after a moment Elfa said:

"It may seem rather surprising, Your Grace, that Caroline has no wish to marry you, but love is more important than being a Duchess, and she would rather starve with Edward than live in luxury with you."

At last the Duke found his voice.

"I admit," he said slowly, "I thought your father's suggestion had already the approval of his daughter."

Elfa gave a little laugh.

"You do not suppose that Caroline was asked whether she would marry you?" she said. "Papa just told her she had to, and fortunately I had prepared her for what he had to say, having overheard him tell Mama how he had ended the feud between our two families."

"Your father's suggestion seemed to be a practical one," the Duke replied, and it was a statement, not an apology.

Elfa smiled before she said:

"It will be a relief to all of us not to have to listen to that endless tirade over Magnus Croft, day after day, year after year, but you will not enjoy your victory unless you marry me instead of Caroline."

"Are you so anxious to become my wife?" the Duke asked, and he did not make it sound a particularly pleasant question.

"No, of course not, although I am not in love with anybody else," she replied. "But if there has to be a sacrifice, it had better be me instead of Caroline."

She saw by the Duke's expression that she had been rude and added quickly:

"I am sorry! I did not mean to offend ... you but you can hardly expect any woman to feel wildly elated at being told she is to be married to a man she has never even spoken to."

"I suppose," the Duke said slowly, "because I have had so few dealings with young girls, I did not expect them to have very deep feelings in the question of marriage, but to accept that their parents knew what was best for them."

"You were young once," Elfa replied, "and surely you must remember that you had very definite feelings then about life, people and yourself. Women are the same, except that perhaps when they are young they are more idealistic than boys."

The Duke was still looking surprised but, as if he felt he must argue, he said:

"But idealistic as you are, you are still prepared to marry me in the most unidealistic circumstances."

"I have thought about it very carefully," Elfa said, "but there is no other alternative: either you marry Caroline, who will be so desperately miserable that I think she will make you feel extremely uncomfortable, if not unhappy . . ."

"Or?"

" . . . I offer myself in her place."

"I have a feeling," the Duke said, "that you think of yourself as a lamb being led to the slaughter."

"Actually I was thinking that you would not do too badly out of the exchange."

"What do you mean by that?"

"While Caroline would only weep and long for Edward, I would really try, although I may not be successful, to be a competent wife."

She thought he looked surprised again and added quickly:

"According to Papa, love comes after marriage, but not with the woman you have married, so that question does not arise between us."

The Duke stiffened.

"I cannot believe your father said anything like that to you!"

"Actually, he said it to Mama," Elfa answered, "when he did not know I was listening."

"So you were eavesdropping!"

"That was how I learnt in the first place what you

and Papa had concocted between you over Magnus Croft."

"I should have thought that to listen to what was not intended for your ears was hardly ladylike behaviour."

Elfa smiled and her dimples flashed in her cheeks.

"Ladies do not have to be 'gentlemen,' and elves have no properly defined code of honour."

"I am glad you have warned me," the Duke said.

Elfa looked at him enquiringly and he said:

"Although I have the very uncomfortable feeling that I am making a mistake, I am finding it difficult, Lady Elfa, to know how I can refuse your request."

Elfa gave a cry of happiness and clasped her hands together.

"You will agree? You really will agree?"

"The only other thing I can do is to turn my horses round and go home."

"Which means Papa will keep Magnus Croft."

"Exactly!"

There was a frown between the Duke's eyes as he added:

"I see now I should never have agreed to this ridiculous proposition in the first place."

"You cannot say that after all the arguments that have gone on for years and years over Magnus Croft!"

"It was extremely unsporting of your grandfather to take advantage of a man who was incapable of knowing what he was doing. I have always understood that when your grandfather suggested the stake, my father thought he was referring to a different piece of land altogether."

"If that was unsporting," Elfa retorted, "I think it much more unsporting when he lost to whine and complain over things instead of writing it off as a bad debt!"

She snapped out the words and the Duke stared at her; then suddenly he threw back his head and laughed.

"Here we are starting the same argument all over again!" he exclaimed, and Elfa laughed too.

"I do not think I could bear another eighteen years of it!" she said.

"Is that how old you are?"

"I am cheating by one month. I shall be eighteen in June."

"You are too young."

"To marry?" Elfa enquired. "Caroline is twenty, but I always feel it is I who must look after and protect her. I do not think it is age in years that counts, but the age of one's intelligence."

"And you think yours is very old?"

"I hope so," Elfa answered simply, "but then fairies, sprites and elves are ageless and live forever."

There was a twinkle in the Duke's eyes as he remarked wryly:

"That is certainly a formidable thought."

Elfa picked up her hat from where she had thrown it on the ground.

"I think," she said, "if you have really made up your mind not to offer for Caroline, you should go on to the Towers. Mama is sitting in the Drawing-Room waiting for you and grudging every moment she is kept away from the garden and her flowers."

"Are you really telling me what to do?" the Duke asked in an amused voice.

"It may seem very impertinent of me," Elfa replied, "but the fact that you have met me here must be a secret never to be revealed to anybody."

She gave a little sigh.

"Somebody might see us and tell Papa, and he will be furious anyway that you are not marrying Caroline."

"Why?" the Duke enquired.

"Because she is his favorite, and now that you have said you really understand, I will tell you that she is very, very beautiful."

"I have already heard that."

39

"Then you know she looks exactly as a Duchess should, and you will be disappointed in me, but it cannot be helped."

"Perhaps I would be wise to stick to my original plan," the Duke said provokingly.

"If you do, I shall somehow contrive to find enough money for Caroline to run away with Edward, in which case there will be a scandal and you will also look silly when it is realised that she preferred a penniless young man to a noble and distinguished Duke!"

"So you are blackmailing me!" the Duke said. "I do not believe you are an elf, but some little fiend who is determined to provoke me."

Elfa laughed.

"You are really thinking about the goblins who live underground and can make themselves very unpleasant to humans if they wish to."

"I remember the goblins," the Duke said, "and unpleasant as they are, they do not look at all like you!"

"I know it will be a great disappointment to you after all the beautiful women you have loved," Elfa said, "to have somebody at the end of your table who will not show the Lynchester diamonds to their advantage. But while I would like to do so, I cannot alter my appearance."

"I dare say I will get used to it!" the Duke said carelessly.

He rose from the tree-trunk as he spoke.

"I suppose," he said, "that Lady Caroline, if nobody else, is aware that when I reach your home I shall not propose to her as expected?"

"You will not see Caroline," Elfa said, "and therefore you have a chance to tell Papa and Mama that you would rather marry me."

"As I am not supposed to have met you, they will think that extremely strange, will they not?"

"You can say you have seen me out hunting," Elfa

said. "I have seen you many times, and thought you looked very distinguished."

"Thank you!" the Duke remarked.

"You are a very good rider, but then you do have the best horses of anybody in the County."

"Are you paying me compliments, Lady Elfa? I am uncomfortably aware that you have manipulated the matter of my marriage entirely to your own advantage."

"And to Caroline and Edward's," Elfa added, "which means you will make a lot of people happy."

"I am naturally rather more concerned about myself."

"Then you must just say over and over again all the way to the Towers: 'Magnus Croft is mine! Magnus Croft is mine!'"

Elfa smiled at him and, holding her hat and gloves in her hand, she walked to the edge of the wood to where Swallow was cropping the grass.

She gave a little whistle, his head went up and he came trotting towards her.

The Duke stepped forward to help her into the saddle, but before he could do so she was mounted, almost as if she flew from the ground on invisible wings.

As she looked down at him and smiled, he saw her dimples.

"Good hunting!" she said and rode off before he could think of a reply.

She was almost out of sight before the Duke had climbed back into his Phaeton and picked up the reins.

Then, as he drove on towards Allerton Towers, he was thinking over what had occurred and found it hard to believe.

* * *

Elfa rode as fast as she could across country.

When she reached the edge of the Park, she found Ben waiting for her.

"Have you given Emily the message?" she asked.

"Yes, M'Lady."

There was no need to ask any more, and Elfa rode quickly back through the Park, into the courtyard of the stables.

She talked casually to Garston as he put Swallow in his stall, then walked into the Towers by a side-door and up the stairs to the second floor.

She looked around anxiously before she reached the landing and was not surprised to see one of the older house-maids coming out of Caroline's room.

"What is it, Dorothy?" Elfa asked.

"I don't know what Her Grace'll say—I don't really-ly!" the maid replied. "It's the second time I've been up to tell Her Ladyship as she's wanted in the Drawing-Room, but she says she's got a headache."

"Has it got worse?" Elfa enquired. "I am so sorry!"

"From what she says, M'Lady, it's reel bad but Her Grace's very insistent she joins her downstairs."

"Tell Her Grace that Her Ladyship will come down as soon as she is well enough," Elfa said. "I will see what I can do."

"That's a good idea, M'Lady," Dorothy remarked, and hurried back down the stairs.

Elfa ran across the landing and opened the door of Caroline's bedroom.

"It is all right!" she said quickly. "He has agreed!"

Caroline sat up in bed.

"He ... has? Oh, Elfa, I have ... been so ... frightened, so very ... frightened!"

The tears began to run down her cheeks as she spoke.

"I know, dearest," Elfa said, "but you still have to go on acting. You know that once he has arrived, Papa will certainly send Mama upstairs for you."

Caroline reached out to take her sister's hand.

"You are ... sure? You are ... really sure that he will not ... change his ... mind?"

"I told him if he did I would find enough money for you and Edward to run away, and that would make him look foolish."

Caroline was horrified.

"You ... could not have ... said such a thing to the ... Duke!"

"I did!" Elfa said, "and I am certain now he will do as he promised and say he will marry me."

"I do not ... think you ... should have done ... that."

"I know, but you and Edward will be happy."

"So very, very happy."

Elfa gave a little cry.

"You are looking radiant! For goodness' sake, Caroline, pretend to be ill, or Mama and even Papa will guess at the truth."

Caroline laid her head back against the pillow and smiled.

"Wait a minute," Elfa said. "I have another idea!"

She ran out of the room into the Sitting-Room, which had been the School-Room, and went up to the table at which they had done their lessons. It still stood in the middle of the room.

She lifted the velvet cloth, opened a drawer and took out a pencil. Then she returned to Caroline's room and said:

"I am going to give you dark lines under your eyes to make you look ill, even if you do not feel it, and for goodness' sake remember not to smile."

"I want to sing and dance ... and most of all ... see Edward."

"I know, but we have to be certain first we have good news to tell him."

Caroline was instantly subdued.

"Yes ... of course, and I shall be praying very ... very hard you are ... right."

"You do that," Elfa said, "at least until the Duke has left the house. Now shut your eyes."

Caroline obeyed her. Elfa rubbed the dark lead of

the pencil with the tip of her little finger; then she applied it under Caroline's lashes.

"Be careful not to rub it into your handkerchief or Mama will see it," she warned. "And be ready to put a handkerchief on your forehead as soon as you hear her coming up the stairs."

"What are you going to do?" Caroline asked curiously.

"I am going to put on my best gown," Elfa replied, "and be ready to go downstairs to receive a proposal of marriage from His Grace the Duke of Lynchester!"

She made a little grimace as she added:

"Reluctantly and under severe pressure, he has no alternative to asking me to be his Duchess or giving up Magnus Croft."

She shut the door of Caroline's room and ran across the landing to her own.

Only as she pulled off her habit and flung it down on a chair did she think to herself that, while she had saved Caroline, she was having to marry a man who was not only very formidable but who would undoubtedly be difficult to manipulate on any other occasion.

She had caught him once, Elfa thought, but it was unlikely she could do so again.

Because the thought depressed her, she went to the window to look out.

The garden was below her and beyond it there was a shrubbery and then the pine woods. All her life, whenever she was perturbed or upset, Elfa had run into the woods.

They safeguarded her, comforted her, and when she was there she felt she was surrounded by fairy people like herself and that somehow she could communicate with them.

It was something she could not explain to anybody else, but the secrets of the wood were very real and part not only of her dreams, but of her life.

She thought now, because she was marrying the

Duke, that she would never be able to fall in love in the same way that Caroline had.

But at least she would always have her secret love, and nobody, not even the man who was to be her husband, could take that from her.

"That is what matters to me," she told herself.

As soon as the Duke had left, she would go into the woods alone to make quite sure that nothing had changed, and *they* would be waiting for her.

Chapter Three

Driving on towards Allerton Towers, the Duke knew that if he had any common sense he would turn his horses round and go home.

He was irritated that it had never struck him before that any young woman would not be gratified and delighted to become his wife.

He knew now after he had talked with Elfa that he had been lacking in understanding—in fact, although he hated to admit it, somewhat obtuse.

He had associated for so long with only sophisticated married women who had flattered him, pursued him and made it very clear that the one ambition of their lives was to become his mistress, that he supposed he had forgotten that other women might feel differently.

As he had said to Elfa, he had not expected that any very young girl would feel deeply, and when the Duke of Northallerton had suggested he should marry his daughter, it had never even crossed his mind that she might have a different view of it.

"I will throw up the whole thing!" he thought, "and forget the idea of marrying anybody for some years."

He knew, however, that this was not as easy as it sounded and in fact was impractical.

To refuse to call at Allerton Towers now would be to insult the Duke in a way which it would be impossible for him to forgive and which would rekindle the feud over Magnus Croft.

47

The acrimony between the two estates was bad enough as it was and had, the Duke had always thought, caused a rift between their employees which was not good for the County.

He knew that his own game-keepers resented it fiercely and volubly every time the Duke of Northallerton shot in the woods of Magnus Croft, and he had often thought that the example set by their masters in quarrelling bitterly over the land should not be taken up by their servants.

At the same time, he was aware that he should not be involved in a matrimonial arrangement which from the very outset was not running smoothly.

Quite a lot of what Elfa had said had both perturbed and shocked him, and as he drew nearer and nearer to the Towers, he felt more and more reluctant to reach his destination.

"The whole thing has become ridiculous!" he thought, but to turn back now would make the situation very much worse than it was already.

Finally, as his horses drew up outside the porticoed front door, he felt almost as if he were going to the scaffold.

It made it no better that there was no one to blame but himself, and he was scowling as he stepped from the Phaeton to see the Duke of Northallerton waiting for him at the front door.

"Welcome, my dear Lynchester!" the Duke said genially. "It is delightful to see you here after so many years when our houses have been barred to each other."

The two Dukes shook hands and walked into the Drawing-Room, where the Duchess was waiting.

The Duke of Lynchester was not to know that there had been a furious row before he arrived.

The Duke of Northallerton had returned, as he had promised, at three o'clock, to find his wife alone in the Drawing-Room.

"Where is Caroline?" he asked sharply.

"I have just sent upstairs to remind her of the time," the Duchess replied.

She spoke vaguely because she was thinking of the large amount of plants she had had to leave in the garden, which needed bedding out before it rained.

The Head Gardener, who was so old that he was past his best, was an infallible weather prophet, and he had remarked gloomily this morning:

"Your Grace'll have to hurry; there's rain on the way. I can feel it in me bones, and too much water can be as bad as too little."

The Duchess agreed with him, but however hard she worked—and she trusted nobody else with her precious plants—she only managed to get in a quarter of those that the younger gardeners had brought from the green-houses.

Her thoughts were far away, or at least as far as the flower-beds, when she became aware that her husband was walking up and down like a caged lion.

"Do not fuss, Arthur," she said. "Caroline is a punctual girl and will not be long."

"Punctual? Punctual?" the Duke enquired furiously. "It is ten minutes past three! When I say three o'clock, Elizabeth, I mean three o'clock!"

"Yes, Arthur."

The Duke walked from the Drawing-Room out into the Hall and spoke to the nearest footman.

"Send a housemaid to Lady Caroline's bedroom and tell Her Ladyship I am waiting for her!" he ordered.

Even as he spoke, he saw one of the housemaids coming half-way down the stairs and sensed that she had a message which would reach him in due course.

"What is it?" he asked. "Where is Lady Caroline?"

The housemaid curtsied.

"Her Ladyship's sorry, Your Grace, but she's got a headache."

"A headache?" the Duke roared. "What do you

mean—a headache? Go back upstairs and tell Her Ladyship that, headache or no headache, she is to come down immediately!"

The housemaid turned round to do as she was told, and the Duke returned to the Drawing-Room.

"Caroline says she has a headache," he announced aggressively, as if it were the Duchess's fault.

"She said she had one at luncheontime, Arthur, if you remember."

"It is only nerves," the Duke retorted. "Just nerves! That is women all over—always making a fuss if they are asked to do anything out of the ordinary."

"I think Caroline has behaved very well, Arthur," the Duchess said. "After all, she did not protest when you told her she was to marry the Duke, though she is in love with Edward."

The Duke snorted and, as if he did not wish to enter into the same argument again, he went into the Hall.

"Come on! Come on!" he said to nobody in particular. "It cannot take so long to carry a message to Lady Caroline's bedroom!"

Nevertheless, he had to wait for quite a while before he was informed that Lady Elfa had said she would see what she could do about it. There was still no sign of his elder daughter.

By the time it was half-past-three, the Duke was in a towering rage.

"Go upstairs and speak to the damned girl!" he said to his wife. "After all, she is your daughter!"

"And yours, Arthur," the Duchess replied weakly.

"Very well, I will go myself," the Duke shouted.

He went up the long flight of stairs to the second floor, and it was Elfa who heard him coming.

"It is Papa!" she reported. "Now act your part, Caroline, and remember, you are doing it for Edward."

"Not . . . Papa . . ." Caroline murmured in a horrified

tone, but Elfa had already slipped back into her own bedroom.

The Duke, finding the climb rather arduous, was moving slowly and his footsteps were heavy by the time he reached the landing.

He knocked perfunctorily on Caroline's bedroom door and opened it at the same time.

"I told you to come downstairs. . . ." he began.

Then he saw his daughter lying on the bed, a handkerchief on her forehead and wearing only her bodice and petticoats.

"You are not dressed!" he exclaimed.

"I . . . am ill . . . Papa."

He could hardly hear the words and, because Caroline was so frightened, they did in fact sound as if she were fading away. Although her father loved her and she loved him, she always found him very overpowering when he was dictatorial.

She was also aware that if he were crossed in anything on which he had set his heart, the whole household would suffer.

The Duke walked nearer to the bed.

"What is the matter with you?" he asked. "This is a fine time to have the vapours!"

He obviously expected a reply, and after a pause in which Caroline did not dare to open her eyes, she said feebly:

"It . . . it is my . . . head."

The Duke was about to expostulate when he noted the dark lines under her eyes.

It struck him that if he forced her to come downstairs in her present state, she would certainly, beautiful though she was, not look particularly prepossessing.

Lynchester might therefore not be as keen on marrying her as he wanted him to be.

The Duke knew all about his neighbour's innumerable love-affairs, and although he did not expect his future son-in-law would be faithful to any woman he married, he had confidently expected that when he saw Caroline he would be struck by her beauty and, for the time being at any rate, become enamoured with her.

The Duke, being a man of the world, knew that most marriages between aristocrats' families were arranged, but he thought it certainly made the arrangement easier for the parties concerned if they had an affection for each other.

Because he himself admired his eldest daughter, he could not imagine it possible for any young man not to be bowled over by her beauty.

It flashed through his mind that it would not hurt Lynchester to wait to meet Caroline, and it might in fact add a certain piquancy to the alliance, which at the moment was obviously lacking.

Aloud he said:

"I cannot imagine a more inconvenient time for you to collapse in this absurd manner, but as I have no wish for your Ducal suitor to see you looking as you do now, I will arrange for him to dine with us tomorrow or the next evening. By then I shall expect you to be on your feet."

"I . . . will try . . . Papa."

"So I should hope."

The harshness of the Duke's words belied the softness in his eyes. Then, because he was extremely annoyed at his plans going awry, he walked out of the bedroom, shutting the door sharply behind him.

Elfa heard him going down the stairs, and when he was out of earshot she ran into Caroline's bedroom.

"Clever girl!" she approved. "You have convinced Papa, and now everything should be plain sailing."

Caroline sat up in bed, taking away the handkerchief from her forehead.

"He said he was—going to—invite the Duke to—dine tomorrow or the next day."

Elfa gave a deep sigh.

"By that time, unless everything has gone wrong, he will have asked for my hand."

Caroline gave a little cry.

"Oh, Elfa, supposing . . . supposing he does . . . not do so? What shall we . . . do then?"

"We can only hope he keeps his word," Elfa replied.

* * *

In the Drawing-Room the Duchess was looking at the Duke of Lynchester with an appraising eye.

She too had seen him out hunting, although they had never spoken, and she had thought he was extremely handsome. At the same time he had an air of consequence and pride which she thought had something conceited about it.

She had learnt from her husband how highly Dukes estimated themselves, and what she had heard of the Duke of Lynchester had not been particularly endearing.

She had loved her husband after she married him, but she had often thought that if she had married an ordinary Country Squire who had been interested in gardening, it would have given her a human happiness which was very different from the life she was forced to live as a Duchess.

"I have often been told, Your Grace, how beautiful your gardens are here," the Duke of Lynchester was saying, "and that the fact that they rival those at Kew is entirely due to Your Grace's inspiration and care of them."

The Duchess's eyes lit up and she felt exceedingly gratified.

She was unaware that it was Harry Sheldon who had told the Duke about her garden, on information which had been given him by his mother, who was also a keen gardener.

"I am sure the gardens at Chester House are very fine," the Duchess replied politely, "and I have often wished I could see them."

"That is something that will be easily remedied in the future," the Duke replied, "but I am afraid they are not as perfect as I would wish them to be and, as Your Grace well knows, improvements and alterations take time."

"That is what I find," the Duchess smiled.

She thought as she spoke that her feelings towards the young Duke had completely changed, and she was sure that any man who liked gardens would be a good husband.

Then she was aware that her husband was choosing his words carefully, and she looked at him apprehensively.

"I am afraid we have some rather distressing news for you, Lynchester," he said to the Duke. "My daughter Caroline, who was greatly looking forward to making your acquaintance, has unfortunately been stricken down with a blinding headache. There seems no accounting for it, as it must be blamed on the weather."

"I am deeply distressed to hear such news of your daughter," the Duke replied, "but actually, I have come not to see Lady Caroline, but Lady Elfa."

If a bomb had exploded in front of the Duke and Duchess they could not have been more surprised.

"Elfa?" the Duke exclaimed. "Why should you wish to see her?"

The Duke of Lynchester managed to reply quite smoothly:

"Because it is Lady Elfa to whom I wish to pay my addresses!"

It took a second or so for the Duke to find his voice. Then he ejaculated:

"No! No! You have got it wrong! It is Caroline you want to marry—my elder daughter."

"I have no wish to argue with you, Northallerton,"

the Duke of Lynchester answered, "but my interest is definitely in Lady Elfa."

The Duchess gave an audible gasp, and the Duke, raising his voice, remarked:

"I do not understand! When we discussed the matter I offered you Magnus Croft as part of the dowry for my daughter Caroline."

"I am afraid I must contradict Your Grace," the Duke of Lynchester replied in an authoritative tone: "your actual words were 'my daughter.'"

"Well, to be honest, I did not think of Elfa," the Duke replied. "She has hardly left the School-Room, and has not yet been presented at Court."

The Duke of Lynchester's lips twisted in a faint smile.

"To have been presented is not imperative when it is a question of marriage."

"But Caroline is suitable in every way," the Duke of Northallerton insisted. "She will grace your table and show off the Lynchester diamonds to their best advantage."

The Duke of Lynchester realised now why Elfa had spoken of the diamonds.

In a way, he could understand the Duke of Northallerton's feelings, which he was almost prepared to echo.

Then, because the argument was becoming embarrassing, he said slowly and quietly:

"I understood that Lady Caroline's affections are otherwise engaged."

Again his words were like a bomb-shell. Now there was a sudden silence, and for the moment it was evident that neither the Duke nor the Duchess could find anything to say.

At last the Duke of Northallerton spoke.

"Who has told you that?"

The question seemed to ring out, but the Duke of Lynchester only shrugged his shoulders.

"Gossip in the country, as Your Grace well knows, is carried on the wind."

As if she felt she should intervene, the Duchess said hastily:

"I am sure if Your Grace really wishes to marry Elfa, my husband will be only too delighted to give his permission."

She glanced at the Duke, who was still standing with what was almost a stricken expression on his face.

"I think, Arthur," she said, "you should send a footman to ask Elfa to come here. I expect she is somewhere in the house."

Without speaking, the Duke turned abruptly and walked towards the door.

The Duchess looked at the Duke of Lynchester, and there was now a pleading expression in her eyes.

"Elfa is of course very young," she said. "She is also a different character in every way from Caroline, and my husband does not understand her. She is very sensitive and I think in many ways unlike other girls."

The Duke was just about to say that was what he thought himself, when he remembered that he was not supposed to have met Elfa.

"I shall look forward to making Lady Elfa's acquaintance," he said firmly.

The Duchess gave a little sigh, as if she had tried to do her best for her daughter, but felt she had failed.

She had always been aware that her younger daughter was different in a manner she did not understand.

Even when she was a baby, Elfa had not wished to be cuddled and made a fuss of like her other children.

Arthur had called her a Changeling, and perhaps that was what she was—a fairy child who had taken the place of a mortal one and was therefore not really human.

The Duchess pulled up her thoughts with a jerk.

What she was thinking was quite ridiculous, and if the girl was different it was her parents' fault and nobody else's.

Arthur had always been obsessed with Caroline because she was so beautiful, and the Duchess, if she was honest, knew that she loved her sons far more than she did either of her daughters.

The Duke came back into the Drawing-Room.

"I have sent for Elfa," he said, "and I only hope Your Grace will not be disappointed in your choice."

He sounded so disgruntled that the Duke of Lynchester found it hard not to laugh.

* * *

"Thank you! Thank you!" Elfa cried.

They had been sent into the garden so that the Duke could pay her his formal addresses when they were alone.

As soon as they had walked down the steps from the terrace onto the velvet lawn, the Duke found himself looking speculatively at the girl beside him.

She had changed from her riding-habit into a green gown that seemed to blend with the foliage in the garden, and she looked, he thought, even more like an elf than when they had first met.

He could not have known that Elfa had first taken down from the wardrobe one of the gowns that had been made for her to take to London when she was to be presented at Court.

It was white, which was considered correct for a débutante, but although that colour made Caroline look like a young goddess, on Elfa it was somehow wrong.

As the Duchess was usually too interested in the garden to be bothered with what her daughters wore, they had been allowed far more licence than most girls had in the choice of their own gowns.

Caroline had a number made by the best dressmakers in London, but with the exception of this gown and one other that was being prepared for her presentation, Elfa had to rely on the nimble fingers of Mrs. Banks, who was the seamstress at the Towers.

Actually, over the years Mrs. Banks had become very proficient in copying designs from the *Ladies Journal* or the gowns worn by ladies who were entertained at dinner or came to stay.

She used to slip into their rooms when they were safely downstairs or out in the garden and would report her findings either to Caroline or to Elfa.

"Her Ladyship has a beautiful gown from Paris, M'Lady," she had said to Elfa about three months ago, "designed by Mr. Worth himself, and if we can obtain the right material it'd suit Your Ladyship as if you'd been born in it."

When Elfa saw the gown in question being worn, she had known that Mrs. Banks was right.

She could recognise the imagination as well as the genius which had inspired Mr. Worth in creating the gown, and she had sent to London for the silk, satin, muslin and tulle, not only for one gown of Mr. Worth's, but for several others owned by the same visitor.

The afternoon-gown she was wearing now was a very good imitation of a Worth creation, and on her slim figure it seemed to float around her rather than hold her stiffly, as her mother's dresses did.

The Duke found himself thinking that the garden was the right place for her.

Then as she said: "Thank you! Thank you!" in a voice of unmistakable sincerity, he found himself thinking that her strangely coloured hair did not need jewels to attract the eye.

"I did not anticipate I would ever be thanked for *not* proposing to a woman," he remarked cynically.

"I will thank you," Elfa said, "when you do propose to me."

"Do you want to receive it formally?" he enquired.

"But of course!" Elfa smiled. "It is something I must write down in my diary and press in my scrapbook for posterity."

The Duke looked at her sharply.

"I believe you are laughing at me, and that is definitely something you should not do."

"Why not?" Elfa enquired. "If you knew the commotion which has been caused over your visit, you would either laugh or cry."

"Does your sister really have a bad headache?"

"No, of course not! And she was looking so radiantly happy when I told her how understanding you had been that I was terrified that Papa would be suspicious."

"I find all this very deflating," the Duke said ruefully.

"I cannot see why you should feel personally involved," Elfa replied. "After all, what you wanted was Magnus Croft, and that is what you will now have."

"And a wife into the bargain!" he added.

"I did warn you I was the wrong one."

"But you promised to make me believe that it was the right choice," he said, and saw her eyes sparkle because his answer had been so quick.

"I really will try my very best," she said solemnly, "but you will have to tell me exactly what you want me to do when I am the hostess at your parties. And as a matter of fact, I have always longed to be invited to one. They sound very much more amusing than the ones we have here."

"What do you know about my parties?" the Duke asked aggressively.

"Only that Mama is shocked by them, and that means they are certain to be enjoyable!"

The Duke laughed.

"The parties to which you are referring will obviously cease to take place once I am married."

"How disappointing! If you are turning over a new

leaf, or refraining from sowing any more wild oats, I must warn you that most of the people in the County are old, pompous, prosaic and extremely dull!"

Now the Duke found himself laughing unrestrainedly before he said:

"I think, Elfa, if that is what we have to encounter in the country, it will be best for us to entertain in London."

She did not answer, and he asked:

"What are you thinking?"

"I was just wondering, as you called me by my Christian name, perhaps I should ask you yours."

"It is Henry Frederick Silvanus," the Duke replied, "but like you, I am called by my last name."

He realised as he spoke quite casually that Elfa was staring at him in a strange manner.

"Silvanus!" she exclaimed.

"Yes, that is right," the Duke answered. "What is wrong with it?"

"He is the god of the trees."

"You know that?"

"But of course! Because the trees mean so much to me, Silvanus has always been a very special god, and I feel very close to him."

She spoke almost beneath her breath, and the Duke looked at her in surprise.

"I must say I have never thought about it like that," he said. "Actually my first governess taught me some classical mythology, but I found Greek, when I studied it at Oxford, rather difficult."

"How could you have? It has always been a language I have longed to learn, but Papa said it was quite unnecessary for a woman. Incidentally, Silvanus was a Roman god, but most of their gods and goddesses were borrowed from the Greek."

That Elfa was surprised at his ignorance was obvious and made the Duke say defensively:

"Perhaps this is a hobby you could take up when you are married."

"I have always planned to learn Greek," she replied, "and also to travel."

"To Greece, I presume?"

"I would love to go there, but even more to the Caucasus, where I believe the trees are thicker, finer and more wonderful than anywhere else in the whole world."

She spoke in a dreamy voice, as if she had forgotten to whom she was speaking.

"I hardly think it would be possible to visit the Caucasus at the moment," the Duke said, "but if you are keen on forests I would recommend Austria, and of course the Black Forest."

Elfa made a little sound that had something ecstatic about it; then, as if she had suddenly come back to earth, she said:

"I am sure such places would bore Your Lordship, but I believe you have very fine woods on the Chester Estate—finer even than ours."

"I have not had an opportunity of comparing the two," the Duke replied, "but I would naturally wish to think that mine were the finer."

She smiled at him and he saw her dimples.

"I shall be looking forward to telling you whether you are right or wrong."

"If you are the sort of tactful woman I have envisaged as being my wife," the Duke replied, "you would of course tell me I was right, whether you thought I was or not."

To his surprise Elfa shook her head.

"I do not believe that is what you really want," she said. "You are too positive a person not to enjoy arguments, obstacles and even battles to get your own way."

The Duke stared at her in astonishment.

"What makes you say that?"

As if she thought she had been indiscreet and given away a secret, Elfa said quickly:

"I was just ... guessing."

"Now you are not speaking the truth. What have you heard said about me that makes you speak as you did just now?"

"It is . . . nothing that I have . . . heard."

"Then what?"

She hesitated, and he had the feeling she was trying to make up her mind whether to trust him or not.

Then he said commandingly:

"Tell me, Elfa. I want to know."

She gave him a glance from under her childlike eyelashes. There was, however, something perceptive about it which told him that what she was thinking was far from childlike.

"Shall I . . . say," she asked after a moment, "I was using my . . . instinct."

"You mean that is what you feel I am like?"

"That is what I . . . know you are like!"

"How do you know?"

"Because at times I do know . . . things about . . . people. It is not something I can explain . . . but I am never wrong."

The Duke was intrigued.

"What else do you know about me?"

"Nothing particular at the moment. When I know things, they come to my mind in a flash like lightning. They are there and there is nothing I can do about them."

The Duke thought this was a very strange conversation to be having with anybody, let alone a young girl he had met only for the second time.

"I suppose," he said, "we should now return to the house. We have been away for the conventional length of time for me to ask your hand in marriage, and for you to accept it."

"I feel I have been cheated," Elfa said, "and I would have liked to put your actual words down in my diary."

"Do you really keep one?" the Duke asked.

"No . . . not exactly a diary."

"Then what?"

"I sometimes write poems," she said, "and I copy down any words and phrases that mean something very . . . special to me."

"I suppose that is what one would expect of an elf," the Duke remarked.

"And also from the god of the trees," Elfa replied quickly.

He laughed.

"I have not written a poem since I was eighteen and fell in love for the first time."

"What was she like?"

"She acted the part of Juliet in a touring company which came to Oxford, and I thought her the most beautiful person I had ever seen in my life. I went to the Theatre every night for a week before I summoned up enough courage to go round to her dressing-room."

"What happened?" Elfa asked.

"What invariably happens in life," the Duke replied. "I was disillusioned."

"Why?"

"She was a very experienced actress, but she was getting on for forty and looked it without the greasepaint on."

"So you tore up your poems, but nevertheless they remained in your heart."

The Duke was about to ask her how she knew that, then thought it would be too revealing of himself.

"I had forgotten until now how foolish I was. I am sure I quickly drank my sorrows away."

Even as he spoke he saw by the expression in Elfa's face that she did not believe him, and he had a suspicion that at any moment he would see her dimples again.

They walked back to the house and up the steps onto the terrace.

The Duke and Duchess were waiting for them, and Elfa knew as they entered the Drawing-Room that her father and mother had been arguing furiously.

She knew quite well what it was about, and the expression of disappointment in her father's eyes was very obvious when, after a few conventional words, the Duke took his leave.

"I have a house-party this week-end," he said. "Then I have to return to London, but I hope we will meet again in the near future."

"Would you like me to send the announcement to the *Gazette?*" the Duke of Northallerton asked. "Or would you prefer to do it yourself?"

"I should be grateful if you would do so," the Duke of Lynchester replied. "When we next meet in White's, we can discuss the most suitable date for the wedding."

As he spoke he remembered that if he was to shoot Magnus Croft, the sooner his keepers took it over the better.

His Head Keeper had complained to him over and over again that the vermin which had been allowed to accumulate there were interfering with their own shoots.

"Jackdaws, magpies, stoats and squirrels everywhere, Your Grace! I've never seen anythin' like it!" he said a dozen times last Season. "We controls the vermin as best we can, but we loses dozens o' pheasant and partridge eggs, while the rooks murder the young birds and there's nothin' the keepers on the Allerton Estate'll do about it."

Now it struck the Duke that if he was to be married, the sooner the better! What was the point of waiting?

The truth was that he was impatient to regain the ownership of the woods.

He was on his way to the door when he stood still.

"It has just struck me," he said, "that if we are to marry in the country, which I am sure we would all prefer, it would be best to do so in the summer, when the garden is looking its best."

He knew as he spoke that he would have an ally in

the Duchess, and before anybody else could speak, she said eagerly:

"But of course! And roses always seem to me to be much more appropriate for a wedding than white lilies."

"Very well, the summer," her husband agreed, "but people may think we are rushing things."

Then he looked at the Duke of Lynchester and added:

"I have a feeling you are wishing to shoot the Magnus Croft woods this autumn."

"The thought had crossed my mind," the Duke of Lynchester admitted.

The Duke of Northallerton laughed, and for a moment his good humour seemed to have returned to him.

"If I can be invited, I will be interested to see how you will drive them. I have always found that the birds go back over the beaters except at Bath Wood, where they fly too high for the guns."

"I shall certainly enjoy trying to achieve a large bag," the Duke said. "What about our fixing the marriage for the beginning of July? Most people will have left London by then."

Elfa saw her mother was calculating quickly in her mind what would be in flower at that time.

"The last week in June would be better," she said.

"Very well then," the Duke of Lynchester agreed. "I am sure we can make arrangements for the ceremony to take place that week, and I am quite prepared to leave it in Your Grace's capable hands."

As he spoke, he bowed over the Duchess's hand with a surprising grace.

Standing in the background, it occurred to Elfa that the one person who had not been consulted was the bride, and she knew even better than the Duke how neglected the woods at Magnus Croft had been.

As it happened, that was how she liked them, and when she rode alone, which was not always easy because of her father's instructions, she would go to those woods and watch with delight the varied birds and animals which she was well aware the keepers described as "vermin."

She knew she would hate for them to be killed.

At the same time, she was aware how ruthless they were, not only on the eggs and chicks of the game-birds, but also on those of the song-birds, none of which could nest in peace in the Magnus Croft woods.

Just as the Duchess had calculated about her flowers, Elfa was calculating for how long she would find those particular woods wild and unspoiled.

"I will slip over early tomorrow morning," she thought, "before Papa is aware that I have gone riding without a groom."

Then she realised that the Duke was actually leaving and her father was walking with him towards the front door.

She knew she should accompany them and walked behind, feeling, as they proceeded down the Hall, that she was almost like a bride's-maid behind the bride and groom.

When they reached the front door, the two Dukes halted and the Duke of Lynchester held out his hand.

"Goodbye, Elfa," he said. "I hope I shall see you very shortly."

Elfa curtsied.

"I think that will be unavoidable, Your Grace."

There was a mischievous look in her eyes that made him wonder whether she meant it was unavoidable for him, or for herself.

A few minutes later, as he drove off, he looked back to see her standing in the doorway beside her father, a slender figure in green.

He told himself that she looked out of place against the formality of the grey stone house.

"She belongs to the woods," he thought and told himself he was being ridiculous and imaginative.

It crossed his mind that Elfa might have been

putting on a clever act as a way of drawing attention to herself when in looks she could not compete with her sister.

He found himself thinking of all they had talked about and said to each other.

Finally he was convinced that however much he might try to pierce the air of mystery about her, she was at least sincere, and what she said was not said for effect but came naturally from her lips.

"It is rather strange," he thought, "that while Northallerton and his wife are quite ordinary and not a particularly interesting couple, they should have produced anything so unusual in the way of a child."

Then he remembered that Elfa had said she was supposed to be a Changeling.

"Of course there are no such things," he thought.

At the same time he knew the idea went back to his childhood's fairy-tales and had stuck in his mind.

"I expect after I have known her for a short while I shall find that her ideas are as banal and commonplace as every other human being's," he thought mockingly.

But for the moment he had to admit that Elfa's appearance, as well as everything she did and said, was certainly most unusual.

Then, as the Duke drove on, he had a strange and inexplicable feeling that he was stepping into a world he did not understand, a world in which he did not believe, which his mind told him did not exist, and which had no substantiation in fact.

Nevertheless he was uneasily aware that as far as Elfa was concerned it was there.

But where or why he could not explain.

Chapter Four

Elfa came slowly out of her bedroom and walked down the stairs to where she knew her father would be waiting for her in the Hall.

She was wondering if he would notice that her wedding-gown was not conventional, but as he was still regretting so bitterly that it was not Caroline he was escorting, she thought it was unlikely that he would look at her.

When she had gone with her mother to London to buy her trousseau, she had been quite determined that she would have things that she knew suited her, and not the gowns that she would be expected to buy as a bride.

She had thought very carefully over the impression she must make as the Duke's wife.

She was well aware that his friends would be surprised that, when he had the choice of the two sisters, he should not have chosen the one who was already acclaimed as a beauty.

Elfa was afraid that their criticism would involve Caroline in some unpleasantness which might suggest to their father that he should try to find another important suitor for her hand.

He had been so annoyed that the Duke of Lynchester had offered for her instead of his beloved Caroline that he had been more than usually disagreeable, and his elder daughter had been included in his disapproval.

This augured badly if Edward Dalkirk should press his suit, and Elfa was determined she would help him and Caroline somehow.

Also, if possible, she wished to prevent people from saying too loudly and obviously that she was not the sort of Duchess they had expected Silvanus Lynchester to take for his wife.

She therefore had to handle her mother very cleverly.

She had gone with the Duchess the first day in London to the shops where the most important gowns were to be bought for her trousseau, and the saleswomen had bowed their appreciation at being given an order for such an important wedding.

Then Elfa had said to the Duchess:

"You know, Mama, that my fittings will bore you to distraction. Why do you not go to Kew Gardens and see what new plants they have there? I believe there are also at this time of the year Flower Shows, which I am sure would interest you."

The Duchess had agreed all too eagerly, only admonishing her daughter that she was not to go alone to the shops, but to take an elderly servant with her.

Accordingly, Elfa had cancelled all the gowns that the Duchess had approved on the previous day and chosen others that suited her own design and colouring.

The wedding-gown at first had seemed an insurmountable difficulty because she had no intention of being married in white, knowing it did not become her.

Fortunately, among the shops they visited there was a young dress designer who not only had ideas of her own but had actually been to Paris and worked for a short while with Frederick Worth.

She had learnt from Worth the methods by which he made his gowns a frame not only for his clients' looks but for their personalities, and she and Elfa had together designed a gown that was sensational. At the same time it was exactly right for Elfa's unusual looks and glowing hair.

Two days ago she had said to the Duke, when they had met at a large party which was being given in their honour:

"Will you give me a present?"

"Of course!" he had replied. "But if you are asking for an emerald necklace to match your ring, you will find there is already a very impressive one in the Lynchester collection."

Elfa had shaken her head.

She had in fact been surprised that he had been perceptive enough to realise without her saying so that she did not particularly like diamonds, and that not only were emeralds her birth-stone, but their colour meant something very special to her.

When the Duke had presented her with a large emerald ring set with diamonds which seemed to glow with a strange, mysterious light, she had looked at it for a long moment before she said:

"How did you know that was what I would like more than any other stone?"

"I am not quite so obtuse as you apparently think I am," he replied.

She looked up at him, and he realised for the first time that, although her eyes seemed filled with a golden light, they were also green.

"The colour is of course very ... significant for me," she said, "and for ... you."

"I am glad I am included," he said dryly, "even if only as an afterthought."

She had laughed and had worn the ring, knowing that the other women who saw it were jealous, not because it was an emerald but because it was so valuable.

Now she replied to his question:

"I was not asking for anything so expensive, but just for a bouquet to carry at my wedding."

The Duke looked surprised and she explained:

"Papa has already ordered the gardeners to do their best with white carnations, white roses and of course lilies. It would be such a large concoction that I doubt if you would be able, when I came up the aisle, to see me behind it."

"What do you want instead?"

"I can make an excuse for not appreciating the local effort if you give me a bouquet of green orchids. I am sure you must have some in your greenhouses."

"If there are none," the Duke replied, "I will have them sent down from London."

"Thank you," Elfa said simply.

Although he thought it was a strange flower for a bride, he said nothing.

Now, carrying her orchids, Elfa started down the last flight of stairs which led to the Hall.

She could see her father waiting impatiently below, and she could also see a reflection of herself in a large gilt-framed mirror which was hanging on the wall at the turn of the staircase.

She certainly looked unlike the conventional bride.

The gown, which had definitely a Parisian *chic* about it, was silver. Decorated here and there with diamanté, which looked like drops of water, it glittered with every move she made.

She might have been a nymph who had just risen from the depths of the lake to move unexpectedly among mortals.

Her veil was also of a very fine silver tulle which Mr. Worth had introduced to Paris a few years ago for the Empress Eugenie.

Instead of the tiara which the Duchess had put at her disposal, Elfa wore a wreath of silver flowers with their centres made of diamanté.

After arguments which had lasted for weeks, Elfa had won the battle not to have any bride's-maids.

"Caroline is taller than I am," she had said, "and if she leads a procession of girls who are the same height as herself I will look ridiculous. Besides, I think it will make people realise that Caroline should have married first, being the elder, and that it is invidious for her to be a bride's-maid."

It was this last argument which had won the day and once again drew the Duke's attention to the fact that his favourite daughter would have a title inferior to that of his second.

Elfa reached the last step of the stairs.

"Come on! Come on!" her father said sharply. "We should be at the Church by now."

"Most bridegrooms are prepared to wait," Elfa replied.

"Nonsense!" the Duke replied. "And if you keep Lynchester waiting too long he might change his mind, and then where would you be?"

"At home with you, Papa! And you would be able to keep Magnus Croft," Elfa answered mischievously.

The Duke, however, was not amused. He merely hurried Elfa through the front door and into the State Landau that was waiting outside.

It was a magnificent carriage which the Duke only used for the Opening of Parliament, but with the footmen standing up behind it in their fancy livery and the horses' heads decorated with white plumes, Elfa was aware that the villagers would enjoy their appearance, even if nobody else would.

The footmen lifted the long train of her gown into the carriage, the door was shut and they started off slowly down the drive towards the small grey Norman Church, which was just outside the main gates.

With an unusual gesture of affection, Elfa slipped her hand into her father's.

"I am sad in many ways to be leaving home," she said in a soft voice. "I have had a very happy childhood, Papa, and I shall always be grateful."

The Duke looked surprised. Then he said:

"You are a strange girl, Elfa, and I do not pretend to understand you, but I am proud of the position you will now hold."

"I am glad, Papa."

"Lynchester will behave with propriety towards you," the Duke said. "He has been a bit wild, and he has something of a reputation—there is no point in pretending otherwise—but he is a gentleman and you will not regret marrying him."

"I hope not, Papa."

"And you must behave as you should," the Duke went on somewhat heavily. "No hysterics now, or making a fuss. A husband has his rights, and whatever he does tonight you just have to accept it."

There was a pause; then Elfa asked in a puzzled voice:

"What do you mean by that, Papa?"

Again there was a pause before the Duke said:

"Your mother has talked to you about marriage, I suppose?"

"No, Papa."

The Duke made an exasperated sound.

"Well, she should have! It is ridiculous leaving you in ignorance. But I suppose she thought you knew."

"Knew what, Papa?"

The Duke seemed to be at a loss for words.

Then as the horses turned through the wrought-iron gates and the Church was just ahead of them, he said hastily:

"Lynchester will have to do his own explaining. God knows, he has had enough experience, and you just do what he wants. Do you understand?"

There was no time for Elfa to answer, and if she had, the Duke would not have heard.

A crowd of employees from both the Estates were cheering loudly as the carriage came into sight, and by the time it came to a standstill outside the Church porch the noise was deafening.

It had been impossible to crowd more than the relatives and a few personal friends inside the small Church.

It had therefore been agreed that those who worked on the two Ducal Estates should see the bride arrive at the Church and leave it with the bridegroom, and then they could either walk, or if they were elderly, be transported in brakes, back to the Towers, where a huge Marquee had been erected for them.

There on trestle tables had been laid out food of every description, and there were enough barrels of beer to keep them drinking and jovial until long after the bride and bridegroom had driven away.

Now as Elfa stepped out of the State Landau, besides the cheers, there were what she knew were cries of astonishment at her appearance.

She smiled through her veil at many of the retainers she knew well, and actually she did not feel the shyness she knew was expected of a bride.

Instead she was well aware that her father was still muttering to himself about what he had said to her in the carriage and, because she found it puzzling, she decided to forget it for the moment and concentrate on what lay ahead.

The Church was packed to suffocation.

She noted out of the corner of her eye as she walked up the aisle several relatives with whom her father had quarrelled in the past, and she was certain they were here today only because she was marrying a Duke.

Then she saw her bridegroom waiting for her and thought that no man looked more magnificent or handsome.

She thought also that he was looking somewhat cynical, as if he found the whole commotion of a wedding somewhat of a bore.

Then her eyes met his and she saw a faint twinkle in them; she knew he was amused at the way she was dressed.

The ceremony, conducted by the Bishop of the diocese, assisted by three other Clergymen, was somewhat long-drawn-out and much more elaborate than if the bride and bridegroom had been an unimportant couple.

The choir was augmented with another from the Lynchester family Church, and they were therefore so squeezed into the stalls that it was almost impossible for the small boys to turn over the pages of their hymn-books.

They sang with a gusto that was commendable, but which Elfa thought was not particularly melodious.

After the Bishop had blessed them, the Duke offered Elfa his arm to lead her into the Vestry to sign the Register, where they were joined by a number of relatives, pushing their way in to show their importance.

It was Caroline who lifted Elfa's veil from her face and swept it back over her head.

"Mama was furious when she saw your gown," she whispered.

"I thought she would be," Elfa replied, "but it is too late now to do anything about it!"

Caroline smiled, and she looked so lovely as she did so that Elfa wondered, as she had wondered before, if the Duke was regretting not asking for her hand as she had originally intended.

She had been aware that the first time he had met Caroline at a family luncheon party, he had stared at her almost incredulously, as if he could not believe he would find anybody quite so beautiful in the country and living next door.

But Elfa was aware that Caroline had looked radiant because she was so happy, and only she knew the tears, the misery and the utter despair with which the Duke would have had to cope if she had been forced to become his wife.

The Duke was in a hurry to leave the Vestry, and they walked down the aisle almost before the relatives had been able to scurry back into their seats.

Then there were cheers outside; an open carriage

was waiting for them, in which they were pelted with rose-petals and rice before they could get away.

"If there is anything I dislike," the Duke said as they drove off, "it is rice being thrown into my face. It stings, for one thing!"

Elfa laughed.

"I know you have not had it happen before," she said, "and it should not happen again, unless I have an unfortunate accident, or die at an early age."

"I hope you will do neither of those things," the Duke replied.

He spoke automatically, but it struck Elfa that if she did die, he would then be free to marry somebody of his own choice and also have Magnus Croft.

It was not, she supposed, the sort of thought one should have on one's wedding day, and she bent forward to put her bouquet down on the seat opposite her, saying as she did so:

"Thank you for the orchids. You do see that a bouquet looking like Harvest Festival would have been very out of place."

"Your gown is unusual, as is everything else about you," the Duke remarked.

"I thought you might approve of it, although Caroline whispered that Mama is furious. I managed to buy it without her being aware of what I was doing."

The Duke smiled.

"You are beginning to frighten me, Elfa," he said. "I have the uneasy feeling that by hook or by crook— and those are the right words—you always get your own way."

"That is not true," Elfa protested. "It is only occasionally I am successful, and I wanted, as the servants say, 'to do you proud.'"

"You have certainly done that," the Duke replied.

They arrived at the Towers and went into the Ball-Room, which was decorated with garlands of white flowers. There were huge vases of lilies beside the small dais on which they stood.

The Groom of the Chambers, who had a loud, pontifical voice, announced the guests.

The relations came first, and Elfa noticed that hers were extremely effusive to the Duke, while his were definitely reserved when they spoke to her.

She found herself wondering how many of them knew or guessed the motive for the Duke's marriage.

Then, after a large number of County dignitaries had shaken hands, the friends from London who were staying in the neighbourhood began to be announced, many of whom had not bothered to come to the Church but had driven straight to the Reception.

"Lord and Lady Dewhirst!" the Groom of the Chambers boomed.

A very pretty woman put out both her hands to the Duke.

"Silvanus!" she cried. "I do hope you will be very, very happy. How could I—of all people—wish you anything else?"

"Thank you!" the Duke replied and raised her hand to his lips.

If Lady Dewhirst's words had not told Elfa this was one of her husband's lady-loves, the critical, searching look she received revealed it very clearly.

There were two other very lovely women whom she suspected of having played the same role in her husband's past. Then she heard the Groom of the Chambers announcing:

"The Earl and Countess of Walshingham!"

This was a name Elfa had expected and, although she had half-anticipated from what she had heard that the Countess would not attend the wedding, here she was.

Elfa saw at once that there was some faint resemblance in her beauty to that of Caroline.

The Countess was fair also, but her hair was the heavy gold of ripened corn, her eyes a deep periwinkle blue.

Her features were perfect and so was her pink-and-white complexion, and from the way she was dressed it was obvious she intended to shine at the Duke's wedding.

Clothed from top to toe in blue to match her eyes, the Countess glittered with diamonds, which she wore round her neck, in her ears, on her fingers and round her wrists, while the bodice of her gown was bespeckled with gems.

She stood for a moment in front of the Duke, looking at him. Then she said in an intimate voice that was meant for his ears alone:

"Dearest, darling Silvanus! I know that we can never, never forget each other at any time and most especially—tonight!"

The Duke kissed her hand without speaking and the Countess moved to confront Elfa.

Now there was a very different expression in her hard blue eyes, and Elfa knew instinctively, as she felt she had known since the Countess's name was first spoken, that she was dangerous.

The Countess did not speak, nor did she put out her hand.

She merely looked at Elfa, and her upper lip curved contemptuously before she walked on.

The Duke, who was greeting the Earl, noticed nothing, but Elfa felt there was no need for anybody to tell her that she had met an enemy and war had been declared.

The Reception took a long time; then the bride and bridegroom went from the Ball-Room to the Marquee outside, to be greeted uproariously by the tenants and employees, who by this time had eaten a great deal and drunk a great deal more.

The Duke made a short speech, which was received with guffaws of laughter; in fact many of the men laughed so much that Elfa thought they would fall backwards off the benches on which they were seated.

They were both toasted; the company sang "For he's a jolly good fellow," to the Duke. Everybody shouted "Long life and happiness!" as they left the hot Marquee and walked to where the open carriage was waiting for them outside the front door.

The guests from the Reception were all gathered to bid them farewell.

The Duke had suggested, and Elfa agreed, that it would be far too tiring for them to drive a long way after the wedding.

It was therefore decided that they would stay the night at Chester House and the following day travel in easy stages to a Hunting Lodge which the Duke owned in Leicestershire.

"I keep some of my horses there," he said, "and I think you will find it enjoyable to ride them, especially around a Race-Course which I have had erected with jumps which are almost as difficult as those in the Grand National."

"I should like that," Elfa replied.

She had a feeling as he spoke that he was not thinking so much about her entertainment as his own, but whatever the reason, it was better, she thought, than going abroad.

She was quite certain it would bore the Duke to distraction to trail round the Museums or Roman remains with nobody to talk to but her.

As if he sensed what she was thinking, the Duke added:

"While we are in Leicestershire I have invited my friend Harry Sheldon to join us. He is an outstanding rider, and we might even get up a local Steeple-Chase, or a Point-to-Point."

"I shall look forward to that," Elfa smiled.

Actually, she had had very few opportunities for private conversation with the Duke since they had become engaged.

They had met in London at large dinners given by ths Duke's relatives or at Balls to which they were both invited, and he had come either to the Towers or to the Allerton House to meet Elfa's relations.

On this occasion he had hurried away long before the other guests, and she did not blame him.

She felt she knew as little about him now as she did before she first spoke to him on the road on his way to propose to Caroline.

It did not take long to drive from the Towers to Chester House, and as they were both somewhat tired from shaking hands and replying to the good wishes of such crowds, Elfa felt there was little to say.

She had been twice to Chester House since their engagement, and she thought it one of the loveliest buildings she had ever seen, certainly older and in far better taste than the Towers.

The first time she had seen it, she felt her heart leap not only from the beauty of the house, but because behind it was a forest of trees which protected it as if it were a jewel.

She had known then that the one thing she wanted to do was to explore the woods, and she felt almost as if they were calling out to her.

But first she had to admire the pictures in the Salons; the crystal and ebony of the staircase, which was a feature of the house; and the priceless collection of china, Greek vases and statues with which the rooms abounded.

But however impressive Elfa found it, her eyes continually strayed to the window, through which she could see the woods standing sentinel and, she thought, possessing a magnetic quality that she had not expected.

Now as the horses proceeded down the drive and the house lay ahead of them, the Duke said:

"I am afraid there is one more duty ahead of you. I have to introduce you to my personal staff; then we can rest our feet and thank God that it is all over."

Elfa smiled at him, but after she had shaken hands at least thirty times, she had been glad to be escorted up the stairs by the Housekeeper.

She was shown into one of the most beautiful bedrooms she had ever seen, which, she was told, was always used by the Duchesses of Lynchester.

It was decorated in the French fashion, with a huge Louis XIV canopied and curtain-draped bed, and the inlaid commodes with their gilt handles and the French pictures on the gold and blue walls made Elfa feel as if she had walked into a Fragonard picture and become a part of it.

The maids helped her out of her wedding-gown, and she rested on a *chaise longue* wearing one of the attractive negligées in her trousseau while her bath was being prepared.

It was then that Elfa began to think of the very strange conversation she had had with her father on the way to the Church.

What had he meant, she wondered, by saying that her mother should have told her about marriage? And the other things he had said about not having hysterics and letting her husband do what he wanted to-night seemed suddenly to repeat themselves over and over in her mind.

Then it struck her that perhaps being married to the Duke not only entailed becoming his Duchess and playing hostess to his guests, but that he would ask something more of his wife.

She had never thought for one instant when she had asked him if he would marry her instead of Caroline that he would expect any sort of intimate relationship between them.

Elfa was completely innocent, for the simple reason that the relationship between a man and a woman had never been discussed in front of her, nor did her special dreams, which were secret to her alone, include human beings with human feelings.

She knew of course that Caroline allowed Edward to kiss her because they loved each other. That was right and beautiful because they were in love.

Elfa had understood Caroline's horror of being married to anybody else, and she thought it was particularly horrifying because Caroline could not bear another man to kiss her.

Elfa told herself that as the Duke had made no attempt to kiss her up to now, he would not change his attitude simply because she had a gold ring on her finger.

Yet she was uncertain. What her father had said made her feel nervous and a little afraid.

There was, however, no time to consider anything but the fact that she must have her bath unless she was to be late for dinner with the Duke.

That, she was certain, would be entirely the wrong way to start off her new life with a husband who, she guessed without being told, was a stickler for punctuality.

She had not missed how everything in the house seemed to be perfectly arranged, with an artistry which depended on a combination of good taste and an insistence on comfort. Flowers and the fragrance of beeswax and lavender scented the air.

"It is all perfect," Elfa told herself, "and he will expect me to be perfect too."

She chose one of her prettiest gowns, which again was green, but a very young, leaf green, like the first buds of spring.

There was a bustle of tulle and a frill of tulle over her bare shoulders, making her skin magnolia white, a perfect foil for the golden bronze of her hair.

She wore no jewellery but her engagement ring, and yet when she entered the Salon where the Duke was waiting, he thought that her eyes in the candle-light gleamed like emeralds.

"You will have a glass of champagne?" he asked as she approached him. "I think you have earned it."

"Yes, please," Elfa replied. "I never expected so many people to come to the wedding."

"They were undoubtedly curious," the Duke said dryly.

"I can understand that," Elfa said, "for there are

few entertainments in this part of the country, except for the Circus which arrives once a year and of course the bonfire on Guy Fawkes night."

The Duke smiled.

"I hope that we have at least equalled such attractions."

"I am sure we have! It will give them something to talk about for the next six months."

"So long? In London we shall only be a nine-days' wonder."

"Because you have married me?" Elfa enquired.

"Because I have married at all," he replied.

"I thought some of the lovely ladies who came from London seemed somewhat surprised," she remarked.

The Duke gave her a sharp glance, as if he suspected she was being sarcastic.

Then, as if she had put him on the defensive, he said:

"I took the precaution of warning those who were likely to be concerned, and if they expected me to run out at the last moment they were disappointed."

"If you had done so, it would certainly have been dramatic," Elfa answered. "Papa did seem a little apprehensive in case you might do so."

"If I did, your father made certain I would not take Magnus Croft with me. He only gave me the deeds in the Vestry after I had signed the Register."

Elfa chuckled.

"My father has always been what the Scots call 'canny,' and it would have been very disconcerting for him if you had kept the deeds and left me behind."

Dinner was announced, and during the meal they discussed a surprising number of subjects which the Duke had never expected would interest a woman.

He was so used when he dined alone with a woman to duel with words which barely disguised the feelings of desire rising within them. Every sentence carried a *double entendre* and every silence meant an exchange of glances that said more than words.

Elfa talked to him of horses, of country interests, and made them surprisingly amusing.

He told her of the places he had visited abroad and found she not only listened with a flattering attention but asked intelligent questions, to which he was glad he was able to give knowledgeable answers.

Altogether he found that he had enjoyed her company in a way he had not expected.

It was only when dinner was finished that he realised that instead of talking to a woman who had just become his wife, he might in fact have been dining with Harry, slipping from one subject to another and finding each more absorbing than the last.

After dinner the Duke and Elfa walked back down the corridor towards the Salon in which they had met before dinner. When they reached it, she said:

"Will we be riding tomorrow morning?"

"If you wish to do so," the Duke said, "and are not too tired."

"Of course I shall not be too tired," she replied, "but I think I would be wise to go to bed now. It has been a long day."

"I feel the same," the Duke answered.

As Elfa hesitated, wondering whether she should say good-night, to her surprise the Duke walked away from her towards the decanter of brandy which stood on a side-table.

"I will not be long," he said, "in case you fall asleep."

Elfa gave him a startled glance, then hurried away across the Hall and up the staircase to her bedroom.

A maid was waiting for her, and as she undid her gown and helped her into one of the fine lawn lace-trimmed nightgowns she had bought for her trousseau, Elfa was thinking about what he had said.

"Shall I brush your hair, Your Grace?" the maid asked after she had taken out the pins.

"Not tonight, thank you," Elfa replied.

The maid obviously expected her to get into bed,

and she climbed onto the soft mattress and noticed that the sheets and pillow-cases were all edged with lace.

The maid, having blown out the candles except for those burning in a small candelabrum at the side of the bed, curtsied, saying as she did so:

"Good-night, Your Grace. I hopes you have a very happy wedding night."

There was something significant in the way the woman spoke, Elfa thought, as the door closed behind her, and suddenly she was afraid.

She had noticed when she was undressing that there was a communicating door which she was aware led to the Duke's bedroom, while on the other side of her room was a *Boudoir*.

Everything her father had said to her was once again repeating itself in her mind, and with it the Duke's remark:

"I will not be long in case you fall asleep."

That meant that he was coming in to see her!

Was it to say good-night? Or did he mean to stay?

Elfa knew that when people were married they slept together in the same bed, but it had never crossed her mind that the Duke might sleep with her, when he had married her only to obtain the acres of ground his father had gambled away.

What was more, as her father had hinted not once, but a dozen times, his interests lay elsewhere.

She had known when she saw the Countess of Walshingham what that interest was, and she was not surprised, because the Countess was very beautiful.

Nor did she blame the Duke if, as he had wanted the land, marriage was the price he must pay for it.

But, Elfa thought frantically, that did not include touching her, if that was what being married entailed.

To even think of such a thing was wrong, because they did not love each other, and she knew now that it was something she could not permit.

She heard footsteps passing the door and thought it was the Duke coming up to bed.

He would undress in his room and then would come through the communicating door into hers.

She looked around, wondering where she could hide.

She could creep under the bed, but that would certainly be a very humiliating position if he should find her there.

Without thinking, she slipped from the bed onto the floor to stand irresolute, looking around her.

There were dozens of other rooms on this floor, but if the servants found her in one of them, Elfa was aware how they would talk and gossip about it.

In fact, whatever she did might easily be repeated to the outside staff, who would carry the story of her behaviour back to the Towers.

"What shall I do? What shall I do?" she thought desperately.

If she had had time, she would have been able to talk to the Duke and explain her feelings. But not tonight, not when they were both tired, not when she had had no time to consider, think or try to understand what her father had been saying to her.

The curtains—she would hide behind them! Then she had a sudden idea.

In the far corner of the room there was a very fine and very elaborate wardrobe. It was not nearly large enough to hold all her clothes. It was there more as an ornamental piece of furniture than as one of utility.

The top of it was heavily carved with angels and cupids, gilded and surmounted by a crown.

From where she was standing Elfa could see that the carving was at least a foot and a half higher than the top of the cabinet itself.

She walked over to it, then, hardly daring to think, driven only by an impulse she did not question, she stood on a chair, and as lithely as she mounted a horse, she lifted herself, almost as if on wings, onto the top of the cabinet.

As she had expected, the top was lower than its encircling carving and, because she was small and slight, she could crouch down and be invisible.

She only wished that she had had the sense to bring a pillow with her.

Yet for the moment she was concerned not with comfort but with being hidden, and as there was plenty of room, she was not cramped.

Then, as she realised her heart was beating not from the exertion, but with a fear she did not really understand, the communicating door opened.

She did not dare to look up in case the mere movement of her head should attract attention, but Elfa was aware that the Duke had come into the room.

She heard him shut the door behind him and then his footsteps, faint because he was wearing slippers, crossed the room towards the bed.

Then she knew he stood there indecisive, surprised to find it empty.

She waited for him to turn around and leave, but instead she could hear the soft movements he was making and realised without looking that he had got into the bed!

Now she understood that he was waiting for her to return, and she wondered for how long he would do so.

There was nothing she could do but wait too, and because she dare not move or peep over the carving to look at the Duke, she very slowly and carefully put her hands together, palm to palm, and laid her cheek on them.

"He will go away in a minute or two," she told herself confidently and shut her eyes.

Chapter Five

Elfa was running and somebody was pursuing her. He had almost caught her when she gave a little cry of fear and flung out her arm to protect herself . . .

She felt a sharp pain and woke up.

For a moment she could not think where she was and sat up, to find she was looking down and the floor was a long way below her.

She stared at it, then was aware that the Duke had raised himself in the bed and, leaning on his elbow, was staring at her in astonishment.

For a moment there was silence. Then he said:

"What in God's name are you doing up there?"

Because she was still half-asleep, Elfa told the truth.

"I . . . I was . . . afraid."

"Of me?"

"Yes."

The Duke sat up a little further, to stare in astonishment at his wife's face peeping over the carving on top of the cabinet.

The candlelight glinted not only on the gold figures but on Elfa's hair, making it glow against the darkness behind her.

"I had no idea," the Duke said after a moment, as if he spoke to himself, "that you would be afraid of me."

"It was . . . what Papa . . . said to me when we were . . . driving to the Church."

"What did he say?"

"That my husband had his ... rights, and whatever ... you did ... tonight I would just have to ... accept it."

"Did you understand what he meant?"

"No," Elfa replied, "but he said Mama should have told me about ... marriage."

The Duke looked even more astonished.

It had never struck him for one moment that any woman who married him would do so in complete ignorance.

The women in his life had always been sophisticated and very experienced in the art of love.

Now he told himself he had been extremely obtuse: he might have guessed that Elfa would be different and that he should have talked to her before they were married.

Because he was silent, after a moment Elfa said in a hesitating voice:

"I thought that ... if I hid from ... you tonight ... we could ... perhaps talk another time."

"It is certainly an idea," the Duke said. "We have not had much opportunity of conversing with each other until now."

Elfa did not speak for a moment. Then she said:

"I did not ... think that when I ... married you you would ... want me to be anything but your ... hostess and your wife in ... public."

"Why should you think that?" the Duke asked sharply.

"Because Papa said your ... interests lay ... elsewhere and I know you are in love with the beautiful Lady Walshingham."

The Duke frowned.

"I cannot believe your father told you anything of the sort!"

"He did not say her name, but other people have hinted that it was she who meant a great deal to you, and when I saw her today I could ... understand what you ... felt."

The Duke's frown deepened.

"This is not something we should be talking about."

"Why not?" Elfa asked. "There was no question of your marrying me because we loved each other, and in consequence I did not expect that you would come to my ... bedroom ... or want to ... touch me."

"You sound as if you would dislike my doing so."

"I do not like people ... touching me," Elfa said simply, "and although I know men and women ... kiss each other, they only do so when they are ... in love."

The naïvety of this remark took the Duke's breath away and, unable to think of an appropriate reply, he said after a moment:

"It seems rather absurd for us to continue to talk to each other as we are doing now, and I imagine you will be a great deal more comfortable if you climb down from the top of that cabinet."

He thought Elfa hesitated, and he said quickly:

"You have my assurance that when you do so, I will not attempt to touch you."

Elfa looked down at the ground; then she said:

"I will climb down as you suggest, but would you please shut your eyes or, better still, get out of bed and turn your back on me?"

"Why should I do that?" the Duke enquired.

He thought he saw her dimples in the candlelight as she replied:

"I am sure that when I climbed up here it was a very improper sight, and I suppose I will look no less immodest as I am climbing down."

"I see your point," the Duke said, "so I will both shut my eyes and get out of bed."

"Thank you," Elfa replied.

She climbed over the edge of the carving, felt with one bare foot for the chair and so onto the floor.

When she looked towards the Duke, she saw that he had kept his word and, wearing a long silk gown, was standing with his back to her, staring down at the fireplace, which was filled with white flowers.

Elfa moved swiftly across the room to the bed, climbed in and pulled the lace-edged sheets around her.

"You may look now," she said.

The Duke turned round.

She was very small and elfinlike in the huge canopied bed, and he thought her strange burnished hair falling over her shoulders made her look like a fairy Princess who had somehow strayed from the woods into human habitation.

He walked towards her and seated himself in an armchair which was placed near the bed.

"I am sure you are now more comfortable," he said.

"I was so tired that I had no time to think of my comfort," Elfa replied. "In fact I fell asleep as soon as you came into the room."

The Duke smiled, and it swept away the frown that was still between his eyes.

"I certainly did not expect to find my bride so high in the air," he replied. "Perhaps the cabinet was the nearest thing to a tree."

Elfa gave a little chuckle before she said:

"It was . . . foolish of me to be . . . afraid."

"But understandable in the circumstances."

The Duke looked at her for a long moment before he added:

"Well, what do you propose we do about each other?"

He was aware there was a wary look in her eyes as she replied:

"I want to do what is right and be a . . . good wife, but being a good wife rather . . . depends on what . . . exactly that means."

The Duke contemplated telling her the truth, then changed his mind.

"What I am going to suggest, Elfa," he said, "is that we get to know each other a little better before we go into any intimate details of what our marriage might entail."

He saw a light come into her eyes and she asked:

"Does that mean . . . you will not . . . touch me?"

"Not unless you ask me to."

Elfa gave a deep sigh which he knew was one of relief.

"That is exactly what I want," she said, "and as I admire you very much and enjoy talking to you, I am sure it will be very exciting doing things together. In fact I think we can be happy."

"That is what I hope," the Duke said, "but if you are afraid of anything in the future, especially of me, I suggest that, instead of hiding, you should tell me about it."

Elfa smiled at him.

"I will do that," she said, "and I am sorry I did not wait and talk to you, as I should have done."

The Duke rose to his feet.

"I think now you should go to sleep again," he said. "And I also admit to being tired."

"We will ride tomorrow morning?"

"Of course," he said, "unless you oversleep."

"I shall not do that," Elfa said. "There are so many things to explore here, especially the woods."

"You have not forgotten we are supposed to be leaving for Leicestershire either tomorrow or the next day?" the Duke asked.

"I suppose we have to go?"

"I am afraid people will think it very strange if we do not," the Duke replied, "but we need not stay long, and when we come back I will show you the woods, which I have loved ever since I was a small boy."

"Of course they are part of you," Elfa replied. "Where else would Silvanus feel at home!"

The Duke laughed.

"Good-night, Elfa!"

"Good-night, Silvanus."

As she spoke she cuddled down in the bed and, almost as if she had asked him to do so, the Duke bent forward to blow out the candles.

Before the last one was extinguished he saw that her eyes were already closed.

"Thank . . . you," he heard her murmur drowsily, as he groped his way back to the communicating door.

* * *

It was with a feeling that she was being wrenched away that Elfa, two mornings later, left Chester House.

She had managed to have a fleeting glimpse of the woods on the previous afternoon when the Duke was engaged with his secretary, and she had found them as enchanting as she had expected, with a magic that made them different from any other woods she had ever known.

There was, however, little time for her to explore them.

She only knew that in them she vibrated to a magnetism that was more insistent and more real than anything she had known before, and she could also hear there the music she always heard in woods.

It was part of the wind in the leaves and in the trees themselves, besides the insistent sound of movement and growth.

"I wish we did not have to leave," Elfa said to herself as she ran back to the house, aware that she had been away longer than she had intended.

Fortunately the Duke was unaware that she had gone out, and she was glad, because she did not wish to explain to him where she had been.

He might question her feelings, and she thought that anything she said would be impossible for him to understand.

Now, driving away behind a team of perfectly matched black horses in a very up-to-date Chaise, she wanted to count the days until they returned.

At the same time, she appreciated how handsome the Duke looked and how interesting it was to be with him, as she had found yesterday when he had shown her the house and the gardens.

At dinner they talked of many things, including mythology, which was a subject she felt he deliberately introduced into the conversation because he thought it would please her.

At the same time, she found that he knew more about the gods and goddesses of the Greeks and the Romans than she had expected, and they argued over the influence that the two empires had had on succeeding civilisations until it was time to return to the Salon.

Wearing a green travelling-gown with a short jacket to match and a small bonnet with green ribbons under her chin, Elfa looked smart, the Duke thought, but still unlike any woman who had driven with him before.

The fact that she appreciated his horses pleased him, and before they left Chester House he had earned her gratitude, which she expressed with a cry of delight, when he told her he had sent Swallow with his horses ahead of them to Leicestershire.

"How wonderful of you to think of it," Elfa cried. "I was afraid you would think it too much trouble to take Swallow with us, and I do want to try him over the jumps on your Race-Course."

"Of course you do," the Duke agreed, "and I have sent half-a-dozen of my own hunters, with which I intend to win every Steeple-Chase and every Point-to-Point."

"I shall certainly try to beat you," Elfa said, "and let me add that Swallow can outrun every horse in Papa's stable."

"That is a challenge," the Duke exclaimed.

They stayed the first night of the journey in a house that the Duke had been loaned by a friend.

It was very impressive, but Elfa thought rather gloomy. There were few trees in the garden, and the countryside around it was flat and uninteresting.

They had an excellent dinner, and once again Elfa thought it was exciting to be able to talk to a man who listened to what she had to say and did not crush her ideas or scoff at her opinions as her father had always done.

When they went up to bed, Elfa realised that, while she had been allotted a large and comfortable room with a big bed, the Duke next door had a very much smaller room, which he obviously intended to use only as a dressing-room.

The communicating door was open and as she saw where he was to sleep, Elfa said:

"If you would be more comfortable in my bed I will change places with you."

He looked at her in what she thought was a strange way before he replied:

"I think you are aware that, as we are on our honeymoon, we are obviously expected to sleep together."

"I thought that was the reason you had such a small room," Elfa replied, "but as I will sleep very well in your room you can have the big bed."

The Duke was just about to say that there was a much better and more obvious solution to the problem when he was aware that if he did so, he would frighten Elfa and also would break the pact he had made with her.

"You forget I was a soldier," he said instead, "and I can assure you the beds provided in the Army are usually small and extremely uncomfortable."

He walked towards the communicating door, saying as he did so:

"Good-night, Elfa. Sleep well. We must start early

in the morning, as I want to be at the Lodge in time
for dinner."

"I shall be ready," Elfa promised, but as the door
between them had already been shut, she was not
certain whether he heard her answer.

* * *

The Duke's Hunting Lodge, which Elfa had expected to be quite small, was in fact a large Georgian
house, and when she saw it she thought she might
have expected that anything which belonged to him
would be attractive and exquisitely furnished.

It was impossible, Elfa decided several days later,
to think of anything that could add to their comfort.

She was just a little apprehensive that when Harry
Sheldon joined them she would be left out of things
and that he and the Duke would perhaps find her an
encumbrance.

But instead she found that, if anything, Harry
added to the enjoyment she already found in being
with an attractive and intelligent man.

He teased her in the same way that he teased his
friend Silvanus and, far from neglecting her, it was
Harry who paid her compliments, praised her for the
way she rode, for her appearance in her new gowns
and most of all, for her quick, amusing remarks,
which added to the sparkle of their conversation at
meal-times.

She was not to know that Harry had said to the
Duke one night after she had gone to bed:

"Your wife has brains, Silvanus, and that is something I am sure you were not expecting."

"Her mind certainly works in an original manner,"
the Duke conceded. "I never know what her reply will
be to any question, and I admit her originality often
surprises me."

"It is certainly a change from always being aware of
what a woman is about to say before she says it,"
Harry remarked.

The Duke remembered that he had complained about this very thing when Harry had asked him why he grew so quickly bored in his numerous love-affairs.

He did not, however, wish to discuss Elfa with anybody, least of all with Harry, and before they both retired to bed, he talked of the Steeple-Chase they were getting up together, about which Elfa was extremely excited.

Harry was far too tactful to ask any questions about their intimate relationship, but he was too astute not to notice that Elfa treated her husband with the trust and simplicity of a child.

But there were no little familiarities between them, which, even with a couple who married without love, somehow became inevitable.

"She admires him; she listens to everything he has to say," Harry pondered to himself. "At the same time she would behave in exactly the same manner with a brother, or even her father."

It puzzled him, but he said nothing.

He stayed a week at the Hunting Lodge, and to Elfa every day proved amusing and enjoyable in a manner which she had never known before.

It was such fun to ride the horses, to race over the fences on the Race-Course and take part in a Steeple-Chase, in which she came in second to the Duke, and a Point-to-Point, which she won easily because the gentlemen chivalrously gave the ladies a good start.

Every day was so full of exercise and activity that Elfa went to sleep as soon as her head touched the pillow, and she literally had no time to think about the Duke as her husband, but only as a man and her host.

It was on the last day that Harry said something which perturbed her.

They had been out riding, and the Duke had left them alone in the Study while he went to see somebody from the Estate.

Elfa, sitting back in an arm-chair, wearing her thin green silk habit and sipping a large glass of lemonade, looked, Harry thought as he watched her, very attractive and as unique in her own way as some of the treasures with which the house abounded.

She was suddenly aware of him watching her and asked, with a little curve of her lips:

"What are you thinking? Have I done something wrong?"

"On the contrary," Harry replied, "I was just thinking that you are right, absolutely right for Silvanus."

"In what way?"

"As his wife, of course."

He saw the strange expression on Elfa's face and asked:

"Are you not aware of that yourself?"

"I do not know exactly what sort of wife Silvanus wanted, and as you know, because he told me that you knew the truth, I was only part of a parcel that contained 10,000 acres of land."

"Yes, Silvanus told me that when it first happened," Harry said. "But I think now you have altered his ideas of the sort of Duchess he thought he would get, which was nothing more than a puppet, a mere cardboard figure."

"At least I am not that," Elfa smiled.

"You are a great deal more," Harry said. "In fact, I am beginning to think you are exactly the sort of wife I would have chosen for Silvanus if he had asked me."

"Thank you! You are very flattering."

"I am speaking the truth! Silvanus, because he is so handsome, so attractive and of course a Duke, has been spoiled by women, and naturally he could no more keep them away from him than he could prevent the sun from shining. But he had been growing more and more cynical and more and more easily bored."

"I shall be sorry when he becomes bored with me," Elfa said, "but then our relationship is very different."

"That is what I was thinking," Harry agreed, "and if you ask me, Silvanus will find his life with you is very different from anything he has envisaged in the past."

"How can you be certain of that?" Elfa asked. "Besides, when our honeymoon is over and we return to civilisation, Her Ladyship will be waiting."

Harry started and she went on:

"I had already learned from Papa that Silvanus had a very special 'interest' before we were married, and when I saw her at our wedding I could understand why he should love anybody so beautiful."

"You do not mind knowing about Isobel?" Harry asked incredulously.

"Why should I?" Elfa asked. "I suppose I shall miss him if he leaves me alone for a very long time with nobody to talk to and laugh with, but I cannot see why the fact that he loves the Countess of Walshingham should stop us from enjoying each other's company as we do now."

Harry stared at her as if he could hardly believe what she was saying. Then he said:

"But surely you realise that Silvanus should not continue his liaison with Isobel or spend much time with her now that he has you? And naturally you should fight to prevent it."

Elfa was looking at him with surprise.

"Why should I do that?" she asked. "If she makes him happy, then it would be wrong of me to make a fuss or try to prevent him from enjoying himself."

Harry was silent.

He could not think what to say and after a moment she went on:

"It would be different if something like that happened to Caroline, because she loves Edward so much, and I think it would kill her if he cared for another woman. But Silvanus is not in love with me, nor I with him, so we are, if you like, friends, and friends want each other's happiness."

"It seems extremely unnatural to me," Harry said sharply.

Even as he spoke, he realised that the reason he found it so strange and in a way shocking was that Elfa was so different from the sort of wife he had expected the Duke to marry and that the Duke himself had intended to marry.

Then the Duke had come back into the room and there was no chance to continue the conversation.

They left the Hunting Lodge and, instead of going straight home to Chester House as Elfa wanted, the Duke decided they should stay the night in London.

He had received an invitation from the Duchess of Devonshire to come to a birthday party she was giving at Devonshire House for her husband the Duke.

"It is a surprise party," she wrote, "and I am asking all my husband's closest friends to make the effort to turn up and give him a specially happy evening."

"I have been asked too," Harry said, "and I feel it is something we cannot refuse."

"No, of course not," the Duke had replied. "Also Elfa will enjoy Devonshire House, and it will give me an opportunity to introduce her to some of my friends who were not able to come to the wedding."

"I hope they will not be disappointed," Elfa said quickly, "and that I have a gown which is glamorous enough for the occasion."

"You had better wear the family emeralds," the Duke said; "then the women will not look at your gown but grind their teeth because nothing they possess is as good as what you are wearing."

He thought as he spoke that many of his ladyfriends had asked him for the loan of items from the Lynchester collection.

He had always refused, first because, having been worn by his mother, he thought somehow it would be

101

an insult to her memory that they should be sported by his paramours.

Secondly, although he had not acknowledged it, he had always felt that they would one day be worn by his wife and nobody else.

"You had better wear the tiara too, while you are about it," Harry admonished. "You will then steal all the thunder from the Birthday Boy."

"I should be quite happy to be inconspicuous," Elfa replied.

However, when she inspected the emeralds on arrival at Chester House in Berkeley Square, she found there was not only a huge tiara which would certainly have looked too overpowering except at the Opening of Parliament, but also a bandeau set with large emeralds of a particularly fine quality and surrounded with diamonds.

Her maid arranged it on the back of her head with her hair falling in curls behind it, and with the necklace glinting on her white skin she knew, as she looked in the mirror, that Harry had been right and all the other women present would grind their teeth with envy.

She was, however, not concerned with what the women would think but whether the Duke would think she did him credit.

She could not help feeling that Caroline, with her fair hair and blue eyes, would have looked breathtakingly lovely wearing the huge necklace of turquoises she had been shown in the safe.

Elfa decided that when she knew the Duke better, she would ask him if it would be possible for Caroline sometimes to borrow some of the jewels, and especially the turquoises.

But for the moment she was content to know that the emeralds gave her confidence, and more than anything else they made her think of the woods.

It was a very short drive from Berkeley Square to

the huge gold-tipped gates of Devonshire House in Piccadilly, and inside a company of the Duke's closest friends was assembled.

The Duchess had said the party was to be a complete surprise, but Elfa could not help thinking the Duke must have been aware that something was up when he saw the house decorated with flowers, fairy-lights being erected in the garden, and chinese lanterns hanging from the trees.

It was, however, difficult to think about the Duke of Devonshire when she found herself being introduced to one after another of Silvanus' friends.

At first they regarded her curiously; then the men paid her extravagant compliments which she hoped her husband appreciated.

Dinner was delicious and long-drawn-out. When it was over, a great many more people arrived and the Band started playing in the Ball-Room that opened onto the garden.

Elfa danced for the first time with her husband.

"I never dance if I can help it," he said, "but as this is your first Ball, people will expect us to take the floor together."

"I hope I dance well enough!" Elfa replied.

The Duke smiled.

She was as light as thistledown and made him feel as if it was not a woman he held in his arms, but a nymph.

They danced a Waltz, then Harry claimed the next dance, and after that there were partners one after another, until Elfa lost count of them and found she had almost to prevent herself from being fought over by those who wished to squire her.

The Duke, having done his duty by dancing with his hostess, then retired to a Card-Room, where he managed to win a considerable amount of money before his opponent threw down his cards, saying in disgust:

"It is damned unfair, Lynchester! They always say: 'Unlucky in cards, lucky in love,' but that is something which will never happen to you. Your Duchess has an alluring face which I know I shall find hard to forget!"

The Duke looked across the table at him in surprise but said nothing.

He merely pocketed the large amount of money he had won and thought it was about time he went in search of Elfa.

She was not in the Ball-Room and he went out into the garden.

It was certainly very romantic with the candlelights edging the paths and the lanterns casting a golden glow on couples in the discreetly arranged seats under the branches of trees or in cleverly hidden arbours.

The Duke walked over the lawn, seeking for a sign of Elfa and thinking he should have perhaps warned her that it was considered somewhat indiscreet for a young married woman to go into the shadows.

He was beginning to think he must have been mistaken and that she was still in the house when he heard her voice and realised it came from behind some flowering shrubs which for the moment blocked his view.

The Duke stood still.

"No ... please," he heard his wife say, "you must not say such things to me."

"Why not, when I think you are the most fascinating person I have seen in years, if ever? I am thrilled by you, my adorable little Duchess, and I have already fallen madly in love with you!"

"That is ridiculous!" Elfa exclaimed, "and ... please ... I must now go back to the Ball-Room."

"I will let you go back on one condition."

"And what is that?"

"That you let me kiss you first."

"No ... no ... of course ... not!"

104

The Duke realised now that the man who was speaking was a friend of his, Lord Hampton. He was a very attractive man and one of the gayest and most sought-after bachelors in London.

He was also noted as being an ardent and persuasive lover and the last person, the Duke thought, who should be with Elfa the first time she appeared in Society.

"How can you refuse me like that?" he heard Lord Hampton say. "After all, a kiss can be pleasant and exciting between two people who attract each other, and you attract me more than I can tell you."

"I do not ... wish you to ... kiss me ... and I want to go back to the ... Ball-Room."

"You are being very unkind! A kiss may mean nothing to you, but a very great deal to me."

"I do not think a kiss could ever mean ... nothing to me," Elfa said, "and when I am ... kissed I am sure it will be ... very wonderful ... and something I will always ... remember."

There was a moment's silence and Lord Hampton said incredulously:

"*When* you are kissed? I do not understand."

"I have ... never been kissed," Elfa said simply, "and so you will understand I would not want ... somebody I do not know and only met a few minutes ago to be the first person to ... kiss me."

She had already finished what she was saying before the Duke realised this was something which could not go on.

He pushed his way past the flowering shrubs and found that, as he had expected, on the other side of it Elfa and Lord Hampton were sitting in one of the arbours.

As he had no wish for George Hampton to realise he had overheard what had been said, the Duke remarked in an indifferent voice:

"Oh, there you are, Elfa, I was looking for you

because the Prince of Wales has just arrived and I particularly want you to meet him."

Elfa jumped up eagerly.

"But of course, Silvanus! I will come with you at once!"

"Hello, George!" the Duke said to Lord Hampton. "The Duchess was asking for you a minute or two ago. You had better go ahead."

"The one person I never keep waiting is our hostess," Lord Hampton replied.

He turned to Elfa and lifted her gloved hand perfunctorily to his lips.

"Thank you for a most enjoyable dance," he said and walked away towards the house.

The Duke said nothing. He only put his hand under Elfa's elbow and walked with her in the opposite direction.

Only as they proceeded into the part of the garden that was not lit did Elfa look at the Duke apprehensively and wonder if he was angry with her for going into the garden with Lord Hampton.

Lord Hampton had been so insistent after they had danced that they should find a place where they could talk together that she had not realised they were in such an isolated spot until they had sat down in the arbour.

It was then he began to pay her compliments and she felt a little uneasy.

Because he was tall and rather a large man, she had felt somehow he was preventing her from leaving him as she wanted to do, and anyway, she had felt it would be somewhat embarrassing to walk back to the house alone.

She had in fact been delighted when the Duke had appeared, but now she thought there was something grim about his expression, and in the light that came from the stars she saw his chin was set at an aggressive angle.

They walked on until they reached the wall which bordered the garden.

It was very high, to prevent intruders, and when the Duke stopped, Elfa looked back to see the lights in the distance and hear the Band playing faintly but romantically another Waltz.

She looked up again at the Duke, who asked:

"How could you have told George Hampton, or anybody else, that you have never been kissed?"

"You . . . heard?"

"Yes, I heard," he said, "and because it makes me look a fool, it is something you will not be able to say again."

He put his arms around her as he spoke and drew her roughly against him; then, with his other hand lifting her chin, his lips came down on hers and she realised how angry he was.

As she had never been kissed, Elfa was not prepared for his mouth to be hard and painful, and for the moment she could think only that he was hurting her.

She wanted to struggle against him, but now his other arm was around her and it was impossible to do so.

Then, because her lips were very young and soft and inexperienced, and the Duke felt as if he held something insubstantial, his kiss altered.

Now it was no longer hard and angry, but instead his lips became gentle, beguiling and at the same time demanding.

He felt Elfa tremble. As she did so, she was aware that the vibrations that she had felt from him had intensified since they had been together in Leicestershire and seemed suddenly to link with the vibrations that came from herself.

It drew them close in a strange, magnetic way she had never known before except in the fantasies in her woods.

Now, as the Duke tightened his arms and his lips became more insistent, it seemed to Elfa that something very strange happened within herself.

At first it was just a warmth that crept from the very depths of her being to move slowly, like a wave from the sea, up through her body and into her breasts.

As the warmth intensified, it became a rapture and she could hear the music she listened to in the woods.

Then it seemed to grow until a sensation she had never dreamt existed arose from her throat into her lips.

It was so wonderful, so perfect and so different from anything she had ever imagined that she could only feel rather than think.

Yet at the same time she knew it was something she had sought but which had always eluded her.

The Duke raised his head, looked down at Elfa and drew in his breath. Then, without speaking, he was kissing her again, kissing her with long, slow, demanding kisses.

To Elfa they seemed part of the stars overhead and came too from the woods and the trees which she knew held the secret within them.

She felt her whole being respond, not only to the Duke's lips but to something deeper and more demanding that came from within his very soul.

Then, when she felt as if they were no longer two people but one, a laugh broke the spell that held them, and the Duke raised his head again.

They came back to earth.

It was impossible for Elfa to speak or do anything but stare at the Duke, as if he were not real but belonged in another world to which he had carried her; it was an agony to leave it.

As if he understood what she was feeling, he looked down into her eyes for a long moment before taking her hand in his. He walked with her slowly back over the smooth lawn towards the house.

Only when they reached the lights and could see the people dancing in the Ball-Room did Elfa say, in a voice that did not sound like her own:

"I would . . . like to go . . . home."

"Of course," the Duke replied. "Get your cloak. I will wait for you in the Hall."

They went into the house, not through the Ball-Room window, but by a side-door and, without even looking at the Duke, Elfa sped up the staircase towards the bedroom, where she had left her cloak.

There were two bedrooms, one opening out of another, and Elfa went to the far one, knowing her cloak had been laid on the bed before dinner and, as a lot of people had arrived since, it might be difficult to find.

The maid in charge did in fact take some time in identifying the short green cloak which matched her gown and which was trimmed with sable.

She found it eventually, however, and put it over Elfa's shoulders.

"Thank you," she said and walked towards the next room.

As she did so, she heard a voice say:

"What do you think of Silvanus' Duchess?"

Instinctively Elfa stood still.

"I do not think about her!" a woman replied. "Silvanus is mine, as you well know."

"But, Isobel, he is married!"

There was a tinkling laugh.

"What does that signify? Most men have to be married sooner or later. What really matters is where they leave their hearts, and that, Audrey, is in my keeping; I have no intention of relinquishing it."

"You are very sure of yourself, Isobel!"

"Of course! And if you are worrying about Silvanus paying too much attention to that strange little creature, let me inform you that he has already arranged to call on me tomorrow afternoon!"

"I thought he was on his honeymoon!" the woman called Audrey remarked.

Again there was that scornful, lilting laugh.

"Honeymoon or no honeymoon, nobody can kiss like Silvanus, and I shall have his kisses and, before he leaves me, a great deal more. I must admit, I have missed him abominably!"

As if she had suddenly realised she was eavesdropping, Elfa stifled a cry and turning, walked across the bedroom in which she was standing to leave it by another door which led onto the passage.

She was half-way down the stairs when she saw the Duke, as she expected, waiting for her in the huge marble Hall.

She went to his side but did not speak. He put his hand under her arm to lead her through the front door to where their carriage was waiting.

Elfa stepped into it and the Duke followed her.

The horses set off and they drove into Piccadilly, immediately turning left in the direction of Berkeley Square.

The Duke reached out and would have taken Elfa's hand in his, but she resisted him.

She knew that he looked towards her questioningly and she said:

"When you ... kissed me ... just now it was ... perfect and very, very ... wonderful, more wonderful than I imagined a kiss ... could be."

She drew in her breath, as if the ecstasy of it were so poignant that it was difficult to speak of it. Then she went on:

"Then when I went upstairs I heard ... the Countess of Walshingham telling somebody that you had arranged to ... call on her tomorrow to ... kiss her! I do not like drinking out of ... somebody else's ... glass."

She knew as she spoke that the Duke had stiffened and was staring at her in the darkness of the carriage.

Then, before he could reply, they had reached Chester House and the carriage-door was opened by a footman.

Swiftly, like a small animal who was escaping, Elfa sprang out.

By the time the Duke had entered his front door, he realised that she had run up the stairs, and he had only a brief glimpse of her green gown disappearing into the shadows.

Chapter Six

Elfa awoke as the maid pulled back the curtains of her bedroom, but before she could begin to think of what had happened last night, the woman said:

"His Grace's compliments, and he asks that Your Grace should be ready at eleven o'clock to leave for the country."

Elfa gave a little start and sat up in bed.

"Did you say . . . the country?"

"Yes, Your Grace, and your breakfast's coming up now."

The maid went to the door as she spoke and brought in a tray on which Elfa's breakfast was arranged.

When she had set it down beside the bed, she started to tidy the room while Elfa stared at the shining coffee-pot, the covered dish and the exquisite porcelain as if she had never seen it before.

So they were going to the country, and that meant the Duke would not see the Countess of Walshingham as arranged.

Not knowing quite what to make of it, she rose and dressed quickly a few minutes before eleven o'clock and went downstairs, to find the Duke in the Hall giving instructions to the servants.

He glanced at her as she reached the bottom step and, as she looked at him enquiringly, their eyes met but neither of them spoke.

Then, because Elfa could see the horses waiting

outside the front door, she moved across the Hall. A moment or so later she was seated in the Chaise and they were driving off in the sunshine.

The Duke's team was fresh and skittish and she was aware, as she glanced at him from under her eyelashes, that he was concentrating on his horses.

She wondered if he was angry with her because of what she had said the night before.

Then, as she felt the memory of his kiss sweep over her like the golden sunshine, she felt again the ecstasy and rapture he had aroused in her and knew that whatever happened, whatever he did, he would not spoil the most perfect moment she had ever known in her life.

She could not explain to herself what had happened; she only knew that the Duke had carried her into a dream which had suddenly become reality.

It was everything that was sacred, personal and intimate which she could never share with another living soul.

They drove on, but they did not speak and Elfa felt in some strange way that they were communicating with each other without need of words.

She knew the vibrations from the Duke were still touching hers as they had done last night, and they were close in a manner that was not physical but part of the magic she had always known existed, but that she had not thought possible to explain to another human being.

They reached Chester House just before one o'clock, and she thought as they came down the drive that the house was looking even more beautiful than she remembered it.

Once again she was sure the woods behind it were calling to her and she could not disobey them.

The Groom of the Chambers greeted them in the Hall and, as Elfa turned to walk up the staircase, she heard the Duke say:

"Her Grace and I will be riding after luncheon. Did the horses from Leicestershire get back yesterday?"

"They're in the stables, Your Grace, and there were no difficulties or problems to report."

"Good! Tell them to saddle Swallow and one of the horses which were left behind here for me."

"Very good, Your Grace."

By this time Elfa had reached the top of the staircase.

She felt a lilt in her heart, first because she was to see Swallow again, and secondly because she would be riding with the Duke.

She had been aware before they went to Leicestershire, and very much more so while they were there, that riding beside him meant something very special.

Yet until last night she had not interpreted the meaning of their closeness except to know that they were attuned to each other in a way that was like the rhythm of the horses they were riding and the music which came to them on the wind.

The maid who looked after her welcomed her with a smile.

"It's nice to have Your Grace back with us."

"Thank you," Elfa replied. "I shall be riding after luncheon and I would like to wear one of my new habits, which I feel must have arrived from London by now."

"They have indeed, Your Grace! And very beautiful they are, especially the silk one which is the colour of Your Grace's eyes."

"Then that is the one I will wear," Elfa said.

Then, because she was in a hurry to see the Duke again, she ran down the stairs and they went in to luncheon.

While the servants waited on them they could only talk conventionally, and yet Elfa felt as if every word they did say had a special and secret meaning.

There came a pause in the conversation and she was aware that the Duke's eyes were on her lips. Because she knew what he was thinking, she suddenly felt shy and the colour rose in her cheeks.

Then almost abruptly, as if he were afraid of talking for too long, he suggested that the horses were waiting.

They rode across the Park, moving the stiffness from sitting so long in the Chaise out of their legs. For Elfa, to be riding Swallow with the Duke beside her was a thrill and an excitement which was reflected in her eyes.

She could not explain it, but the sensations the Duke had aroused last night were still rising within her, and she knew that every time she looked at him and was aware how handsome and magnificent he was her heart seemed to behave in a very strange fashion.

Because it was very hot, they soon slowed their horses into an easy trot, then into a walk as the Duke led the way into a wood on the edge of the Park.

There was a ride through the fir trees that was out of the sun, and yet because the tops of the trees were gold with the radiance of it, Elfa felt as if they were in a tunnel of light.

The wood was very quiet except for the occasional bird that rose into the sky at their approach, and yet Elfa was sure the trees were speaking to them. Although it seemed impossible, she felt the Duke could hear them as she did.

They rode for a long way, and only when the wood ended did the Duke lead the way back through the trees, along a narrow, twisting, mossy path, which to Elfa was so beautiful that she wanted to stop and feel that the spirits of the wood were close to them.

She was, however, too shy to suggest it to the Duke and they rode on until once again they could see the house. She knew that he intended to go back because he had a plan for them both already in his mind.

She had realised that she could read his thoughts and she felt too that he could read hers. As if she had asked the question, he said:

"I brought you here this afternoon because this is a wood where I often ride when I am alone. Tomorrow or perhaps later this evening, I will take you to the wood behind the house, where there is a very special place I wish you to see."

"Special for you?" she asked.

"Very special," he answered, "and I think you will be able to explain to me why it meant so much when I was a child and later a youth."

He smiled before he went on:

"When I was in trouble, when I felt lonely or when I needed comfort in some way I could not explain to myself, I went to the pool in the centre of the wood."

"A pool?" Elfa asked.

"I am sure you will tell me it is magic," the Duke said, "and although I have not visited it for many years, it now is, since I have met you, vividly in my mind."

The way he spoke made Elfa feel suddenly breathless, but they said no more until they reached the house, where the grooms were waiting for them.

Elfa went upstairs to change, and now, because she felt as if it was important, she put on one of her green gowns that she had chosen specially because she thought the Duke might admire her in it.

She looked at the clock as she did so and realised it was later than she had thought, and that they had ridden for a long time.

She was not in the least tired, but instead felt vividly alive in a way that made her feel almost as if she flew down the stairs into the Salon, where she knew the Duke would be waiting for her.

She was not mistaken.

He was there, very elegantly dressed, having changed from his riding-clothes, but at the same time looking cool and relaxed. Also, although she might have been mistaken, he appeared happier than he had ever looked before.

Tea was waiting, and because she knew he would expect it, Elfa went to the table to pour out of a large Georgian silver teapot.

There were a great number of delicacies to choose from, but while the Duke accepted a cup of tea, he ate nothing and Elfa also found she had no wish to eat.

Although she had felt thirsty when they were riding, it was an effort even to sip the fragrant China tea.

"I want to talk to you, Elfa," the Duke said in his deep voice, "but perhaps because we have had a busy day I should let you rest."

"I am not tired," Elfa replied, "and I have no . . . wish to . . . rest."

"Then shall we talk here?" he asked, putting down his empty cup, "or shall we go into the Study, which I feel somehow is more intimate?"

"I would like to go into the Study," Elfa answered, "and I know because you have your pictures of horses there it is the room you like the best."

"How do you know that?" he asked. Then he smiled. "I think without any explanations we know a great deal about each other."

Elfa drew in her breath.

There was an expression in the Duke's eyes that made her feel as if she were standing on top of a cliff. One step more and she would be floating away into an indefinable space, and she had no idea where she would land.

"Elfa," the Duke said suddenly, and he put out his hand towards her.

As he did so, the door of the Salon opened, there was the sound of chattering voices and the Butler announced:

"The Countess of Walshingham, Major and Mrs. Fenwick, Mr. Harry Sheldon, Lord Hampton!"

Before the Butler had finished his announcement the Countess was proceeding down the room with her hands outstretched towards the Duke, her eyes sparkling, her red lips smiling.

"Are you surprised to see us, Silvanus?" she asked. "When I heard you had left London without telling me, I decided you should not escape so easily! So we have all come to stay with you."

For a moment the Duke seemed speechless.

Then, as the Countess held his hands and stood smiling up at his face, looking so beautiful that Elfa felt no man could resist her, the Duke's eyes met Harry Sheldon's.

"It was not my idea!" Harry said, as if he had been asked the question. "Isobel insisted on coming, and I thought I should come too to give you moral support."

"Of course I insisted," Isobel interposed. "You have always told me that any house you own is at my disposal, and now I am keeping you to that promise. Besides, Kitty was longing to see you again."

As if with an effort, the Duke remembered his manners and held out his hand to Mrs. Fenwick.

"Nice to see you, Kitty!" he said. "How are you, Edward?"

He was aware as he did so that Lord Hampton was already at Elfa's side, raising her hand to his lips.

"I intended to call on you today, Duchess," he said, "and you see, although you eluded me, I have caught up with you."

The Duke interrupted, saying:

"Elfa, I do not think you have met Mrs. Fenwick, who is an old friend of mine, while her husband and I were in the same Regiment."

Elfa shook hands with them, but made no attempt to greet the Countess, who was looking only at the Duke in a manner that Harry thought was extremely embarrassing.

Then Elfa said in a voice that sounded softer and quieter than those of the uninvited guests:

"I think that if your friends are staying here, Silvanus, I should tell the Housekeeper of their arrival."

The Duke knew it was an excuse to leave the Salon and he said quickly:

"Yes, do that."

"There is no need for the Duchess to take upon herself to make such arrangements," the Countess said sharply. "Mrs. Field is well aware which is *my* room, and I have already told the Butler where the rest of the party will sleep."

Elfa behaved as if she had not heard and, as she moved away from the Duke's side, Harry hurried ahead to open the door for her.

She stopped to say to him:

"I am glad to tell you the horses arrived home safely and were none the worse, either for the journey or for the hard exercise we gave them."

"I am delighted to hear that," he said.

He thought of following her into the Hall and apologising to her, but he was not quite certain if she would think he was interfering.

He had in fact been horrified when he had received a message from Isobel telling him that she intended to take a party of friends to Chester House and inviting him to come with them.

Although the Duke had said nothing to him, he had suspected, because they were such close friends, that Silvanus was not as much interested in Isobel as he had been before his marriage.

In fact, he would have been prepared to bet a large amount that during the time the Duke had been with Elfa in Leicestershire he had hardly given her a thought.

Harry, however, had warned the Duke that Isobel would fight like a lioness to keep what she believed to be hers, and he was quite sure that the one person who would suffer would be Elfa. But he had no idea how he could prevent it.

Then, as he wondered what he should do, he was aware that Elfa was walking slowly and gracefully up the stairs, but not as if she were running away from anything unpleasant.

There was no time to do anything or for anybody to have an intimate discussion before it was time to change for dinner.

When Elfa had gone to her bedroom, making no effort to get in touch with the Housekeeper, she found her maid was already there, unpacking the things which had come from London and laying out her evening clothes.

Elfa went to the window, to stand looking out at the shadows deepening on the lawn and beneath the trees in the Park.

Her thoughts were far away from the woman downstairs, and she knew that the Duke had not only been surprised by the Countess's arrival but also resentful.

Elfa knew him well enough by now to know that he disliked his plans being changed or altered and, because he was a perfectionist, surprises were something he considered disruptive and seldom pleasant.

Deliberately Elfa thought of their ride in the woods and the feeling of closeness which even now she had not lost.

"What will you wear this evening, Your Grace?" the maid asked behind her, and for a moment it was impossible for her to concentrate on the question.

Then somehow the decision seemed to be made for her.

"I will wear my wedding-gown!"

* * *

Looking down the table at his wife sitting at the other end of it, with Lord Hampton on her right and Harry on her left, the Duke had the feeling that Elfa

121

had withdrawn into a world of her own, and he was suddenly afraid that he would not be able to reach her.

All through the meal he was aware that Isobel was being both provocative and aggressive, except to himself, to whom she was being over-affectionate and over-demonstrative.

He had known when he entered the Salon before dinner and she had swept towards him with a smile on her lips, her hands going out to touch him caressingly, that his feelings had completely changed and he no longer even found her beautiful.

It was not unusual for him to become bored with the women who had attracted him, but usually there was a slow cooling-off period, when he found their mannerisms irritating and their conversation banal. Even though they still had the power to arouse him physically, mentally they began to make him yawn.

Now, almost as if a curtain had fallen between him and Isobel, he found her beauty had no power to move him even to a grudging admiration.

As dinner progressed, he began to dislike her possessive manner, the venom of her wit, and the way in which she tried to monopolise everybody's attention, especially his own.

He kept looking at Elfa and wondering what she was thinking and feeling.

He regretted now that he had not had the strength of mind or the ruthlessness to have refused to accept the party of friends he had not invited and had had no intention of entertaining.

He had realised, however, that to do so would have caused a scandal which would have reverberated through the Clubs and put not only himself but also Elfa in a bad light.

There really had been nothing he could do but accept them and when, as they went up to dress, Harry had muttered an apology beneath his breath, the Duke, surprisingly, had merely said:

"It was my fault. I should have anticipated this might happen."

"I did warn you what Isobel was like," Harry said

"I know, but I did not believe you. Unfortunately, you were right."

Harry would have said something else, but Isobel, who was walking up the stairs ahead of them with her arm through Kitty Fenwick's, turned back to ask:

"What are you two whispering about? You know, darling Silvanus, that I do not allow you to have any secrets from me."

The Duke had not replied. He had merely gone into his own bedroom and slammed the door.

He was aware that what Isobel referred to as "her bedroom" was the one opposite his own.

He knew why she had come and what she intended, and it made him extremely bad-tempered as his valet helped him into his evening-clothes.

There were so many things he wanted to say to Elfa, and he had planned to do so after dinner.

But now, as the meal dragged on, he wondered how the evening would end and what he could do to prevent Isobel from insulting his wife, which she was doing with every word she spoke, with every look she gave him and every time her hands touched him with a familiarity which he resented more each time.

At last, when it was time for the ladies to leave the room, Elfa looked down the table to catch the Countess's eye before she rose to her feet, but Isobel rose first, saying, as if she were the hostess:

"I suppose we have to leave the gentlemen to their port, but Silvanus, darling, do not be too long. You know how I hate you not being with me."

It was so outrageous that even Harry gasped, but Elfa walked towards the door, to stand there waiting for Isobel to leave first.

She swept past her in a flitter of blue chiffon and glittering diamonds and Kitty Fenwick followed her.

As they walked side by side along the corridor with Elfa behind them, Isobel said:

"I expect you know I am helping Silvanus to improve the house and rearrange his treasures."

"I have never seen such magnificent paintings!" Kitty replied.

"Almost as magnificent as the owner of them!" Isobel smiled.

They walked into the Drawing-Room and the Countess said:

"I cannot allow anybody to sit in my favourite chair, which of course is always kept for me, but sit beside me, Kitty, and I will tell you an exciting idea I have."

"What is that?" Kitty Fenwick asked.

"I expect you have heard that Silvanus has built himself a new yacht?" Isobel said. "I have not seen it yet, but I believe it is quite fantastic. When it is ready, we must arrange a trip abroad, and I do not see why, instead of going to Scotland, Silvanus should not take us up the Seine. Can you imagine anything more romantic than to be in Paris with him?"

The Countess was speaking loudly, to make sure that Elfa should hear exactly what she was saying, but instead of listening, Elfa had gone to the open window to look out into the garden.

Suddenly, without even glancing at the two women seated by the flower-filled fireplace, she stepped out onto the terrace and disappeared.

* * *

The Duke refused to linger over the port and rose to leave the table.

"What is the hurry, Silvanus?" Lord Hampton asked.

The Duke did not reply, and only Harry knew that the reason for his urgency was that he was afraid of what Isobel was saying to Elfa.

They reached the Drawing-Room, Lord Hampton

carrying a full glass of port with him, to find only Isobel and Kitty.

The Duke did not need to ask where Elfa was.

It was almost as if the open window told him the answer, or perhaps the way he had begun to know what she was thinking made his vibrations respond to those she had left behind.

Just as she had done, without any explanation, he walked out onto the terrace.

Only as Isobel realised what he was about to do and cried out his name did he hurry down the steps into the garden and move quickly across the velvet lawn.

It had been hot all day and it was even hotter now. There was not a breath of wind to cool the heat, which was just as intense as if the sun were still shining.

Stars filled the sky and there was a moon rising over the wood, which was where the Duke was certain he would find Elfa.

There was, however, a large expanse of the garden to go through first, and because he was walking quickly, feeling an urgency to be with her, he pulled off his tight-fitting coat and walked on, holding it over his arm.

The lawns came to an end, and now there was a path between low shrubs in bloom, which passed on through larger ones until it reached the wood.

As he came to the trees, the Duke realised how hot he was, and he threw the coat he carried down on the ground, thinking he would pick it up on his return.

On an impulse he undid his tie, then his shirt, and pulled it off.

It was something he had often done in hot weather when he was a boy, and it was an action that had been frowned upon by his Governesses and later by his Tutors. But it had seemed right at the time and seemed right now.

As he walked on unencumbered, it might have been

125

difficult for him to find his way but for the shafts of moonlight shining silver through the trees.

The wood looked so beautiful that he wanted, as he had never wanted anything before, to share its loveliness with Elfa, knowing how much the mystic beauty that was of a very different world from the one he had left would mean to her.

He was sure the path he was following would lead him to her, for it never struck him that it might have been difficult for her to find her way in a wood where she had never been before.

When finally he came to the place where he was certain she would be, it was inevitable that she should be there.

There was a clearing, and high trees encircled the pool which he had told Elfa had always meant something special to him as a boy.

There were water lilies in it and kingcups growing round the edge. On one side, where the trees did not encroach quite so closely, there was a patch of thick green grass interspersed with wild flowers.

It made the pool seem more mysterious and fairy-like.

There were trees that towered high, dark and protecting, and the first thing that the Duke saw between Elfa and himself was what appeared to be a dazzling shaft of moonlight, not pointing up in the air towards the moon, but shining on the ground beside the pool.

Then, at a second glance, he realised that it was Elfa's gown, which she had worn at dinner, and that she was standing naked.

He stood still, looking at her, while the moonlight on her body made her appear immortal, a nymph from the water, from which he realised she had just emerged.

She was very slight and slender and lovely, although he did not feel for the moment that she was a woman whom he desired.

Instead she was something ethereal to which he responded not with his body, but with his spirit and the very breath he drew.

As if Elfa felt his presence without seeing him, she turned her head and looked at him as he stood in the shadows of the trees.

Then, as he walked towards her, she did not move or make any effort to hide her nakedness.

She only stood with the moonlight glinting on the drops of water on her body and waited.

He reached her side and stood looking at her, feeling as if they reached for each other across eternity and that everything that was happening had been ordained, perhaps long before they were born.

Then the Duke heard the music which seemed to come not only from the trees which overshadowed them, but from Elfa herself.

It was as if they moved to the melody of it and, very slowly, as time stood still, he put his arms around her and pulled her close against him.

She felt cool and insubstantial as his lips found hers.

For the moment there was no passion in his kiss, only a reverence, as if he touched something sacred and spiritual that was as eternal as God, and part of their souls.

Then as he felt Elfa's body against his bare skin becoming warm and more human, his kiss deepened.

He knew, as she quivered against him, that he had evoked the same ecstatic rapture she had felt last night and which he had felt too.

Never in his life, in all the times he had made love to innumerable women, had he ever known such feelings as Elfa had aroused in him when they had kissed in the garden of Devonshire House.

Because it had been so strange and so wonderful, he had this morning almost doubted that it could have occurred and believed he must have imagined it.

Now he knew it was only a very small part of what she could make him feel and the wonder they could find together.

He drew her closer and closer, and the mystery of the night was in them and in a love which was different from any love the Duke had ever known or even imagined.

Elfa was already his and he was hers; they were indivisible. At this moment they were as gods, yet he was still a man.

The moonlight was dazzling; the music of the trees rose louder and came also from their hearts; the spirits of the wood were waiting.

The Duke picked Elfa up in his arms and felt as if he held a piece of thistledown against his heart, before he laid her gently down on the grass.

There was the scent of flowers, but it was not only of their fragrance that he was aware, but that everything around them, from the earth to the trees, was living and breathing; he could feel their life pulsating through him.

It was part of the music, the moonlight, the stars and Elfa.

Then there was only the glory that swept them on the shimmering wings of ecstasy up into the sky, and they were one. . . .

* * *

A long time later, when the light of the moon had moved from the pool and the shadows of the trees covered them protectingly, Elfa whispered:

"I . . . love . . . you!"

Her voice was faint, and it was in fact the first time she had spoken since the Duke came to her. Yet he felt as if they had said a million things to each other, and there were no longer any secrets between them.

"And I love you, my perfect Elf, my darling, my heart, my whole life!" he replied.

"I did not . . . know I could feel . . . anything so exciting, so . . . glorious . . . so absolutely perfect, and yet still be . . . alive!"

"I did not frighten you?"

He knew her lips curved in a smile before she answered:

"How could I be . . . frightened of . . . Silvanus?"

"Is that who you thought I was?"

"You are the god I have always . . . worshipped and . . . searched for . . . amongst the trees . . . and when you came to me just now I did not think you were you . . . but Silvanus. I should really have knelt at your feet."

"As I should have knelt at yours," the Duke said, "because you are the most exquisite nymph that ever came from a magic pool in a secret wood."

Elfa gave a little laugh that was one of sheer happiness.

"A pool of magic," she said, "and when I saw it I knew why you had come here when you were a boy."

"You knew I would follow you here tonight?"

"I think I must have known it," she said; "the trees have called me ever since I first saw them, and I knew they were compelling me to come to them. When I reached the wood they . . . showed me where to . . . go."

"I thought that must have been what happened," the Duke said.

"Oh, Silvanus! You do understand!" Elfa cried. "I never thought or dreamt that anyone would understand, least of all you."

She felt him stiffen instinctively.

"I do not mean that unkindly . . . but because of the things I have heard about you, I thought of you only as a man . . . a very magnificent one, but still just . . . a man."

"And now?"

"To me you are . . . the god who has always been . . . part of my life."

129

"As you have been part of mine, although I was completely unaware of it," the Duke said. "Just as now when I took you in my arms I was sure that not only this had been ordained since the beginning of time, but also that we will be together for all eternity."

"Do you mean . . . that?"

"It will take a lifetime for me to convince you that I am sincere," the Duke replied, "but ever since I first saw you, your face has haunted and enchanted me, and I know that now no other woman could ever attract me."

Elfa gave a little cry of happiness and pressed herself against him.

The Duke ran his hand down the long line of her hip before he said:

"Why should I say 'other woman'? You are not a woman; you are a supernatural being whom I find bewitching and irresistibly enchanting."

"I . . . want you to . . . feel like . . . that."

"Why do you want me to feel like that?"

"Because," she whispered, "I had no idea that love could be so . . . compelling . . . so thrilling . . . so overpowering."

She pressed herself a little nearer to the Duke as she went on:

"It is magic . . . the magic that I have felt amongst the trees . . . heard in the music of the leaves and listened to when they . . . spoke to me."

"We will listen to them together," the Duke said, "then we shall never make mistakes."

"I was mistaken about you . . . but now I will love and worship you forever!"

The way she spoke was very moving and the Duke's lips found hers.

His kiss was gentle, and yet demanding.

As he felt her body soft and warm beneath his hands, as he heard the music around them growing deeper and louder, he could feel once again the life from the flowers, the trees and the earth pulsating through them, making them a part of all creation.

His lips became more insistent and possessive; he could feel the fire rising within him and he knew as Elfa's body quivered against his that little flames were flickering in her.

"Love me! Oh, Silvanus . . . love me!" she cried.

Then the light that came from them both was as dazzling as the moonlight, and their love lifted them up to the stars.

Chapter Seven

The Duke awoke with an irrepressible feeling of happiness.

He lay for a moment with his eyes closed, thinking that never in his life had he felt not only so happy, but so satisfied and complete.

Then he opened his eyes and was aware that the curtains were drawn back: presumably he had not heard his valet coming to call him, and he must have left him to sleep on.

It was not surprising, because it was only when the stars were fading in the sky and the moon was a pale shadow of herself that he and Elfa had come back to the house.

It had been an agony to tear themselves away from the enchantment of the pool and to know they must leave their secret world for reality.

Elfa had, as they turned to go back through the wood and into the garden, looked up at him with such an expression of love in her eyes that he had thought nobody could be so alluring and still be human.

There was nothing here to jar or disrupt them, and only the house, lightless and silhouetted against the sky, made the Duke remember that tomorrow there would be problems, although neither of them could ever forget tonight.

He took Elfa in through a side-door and they went up a secondary staircase without seeing the night-watchmen or the footman on duty.

He had taken off her gown and lifted her onto the bed, thinking as she lay with her hair glowing gold against the pillow that he had been truthful when he had said that he could never look at another woman, or find one attractive.

"Go to sleep, my darling," he had said as he bent over her, "thinking only that we have found each other and nothing else is of any importance."

"I love you ... Silvanus ... I love you!" Elfa murmured.

He kissed her very gently on the lips and she was asleep before he left the room.

Alone, he found himself saying, as he had not done for many years, a prayer of gratitude and thankfulness, for after all the times he had been disappointed and disillusioned by women he had found the one who was the other half of himself.

He had fallen asleep with Elfa's name on his lips, and now he felt a surge of excitement pulsate through his body because she was near him and in a few seconds he would see her.

He looked at the clock and thought she too would have slept as deeply as he had, so that he could waken her with a kiss.

Then, as he stepped out of bed, he saw something white beneath the communicating door of their rooms.

He had shut it last night because he had thought that when he was called it might awaken Elfa, and he knew that, for perhaps the first time, he was thinking only of the woman he loved and not himself.

It was for the same reason that he had gone to his own room after lifting her into bed and resisted a desire to hold her for the rest of the night in his arms.

Although to have wakened her to womanhood had been a rapturous experience, unlike anything he had known or imagined, he knew that for her its glory and wonder had also been deeply emotional, and he must be very gentle and tender with her.

"I will protect her and look after her all my life," the Duke had vowed.

He had then realised that she had given him back the ideals he had lost when he grew older and had awakened many others of which until now he had been unaware.

Now, as he bent to pick up the letter which had been pushed under the door, he was suddenly afraid.

What had happened? Why had she written to him when she only had to turn the handle to be in his arms?

He thought, although it was absurd, that his hand was shaking as he drew a single sheet of paper from the envelope.

Elfa had written only a few lines and he read them slowly:

I love you, Silvanus! I could not bear anything to spoil or hurt the wonder of our love. When you call me I shall hear you and come back.

Even as he read what she had written, the Duke understood.

He felt the same and he knew their love for each other was so divine that it would be sacrilege for it to be damaged or soiled in any way, and the one person who could do that was Isobel.

He understood exactly what Elfa was feeling, but it worried him as to where she had gone and how.

Although she said they were so closely attuned that he could call her back to him, he could not bear to be apart from her even for a few hours.

He stood holding the letter in his hand, and just as he had planned the deployment of his troops as a soldier, and similarly had planned his houses and estates to bring them to perfection, so what he must now do seemed to drop into place as if it were written down in front of his eyes.

Thinking with a concentration that came from years of self-control and of exercising his intelligence, the Duke walked across the room to ring the bell.

When his valet answered, he started to give his orders, sharply, clearly and with an insistence which surprised those who listened to him.

* * *

An hour later the Duke was riding very swiftly across country towards Northallerton Abbey.

Because he was on one of the fastest horses he had ever owned, it took him less than twenty minutes, and when he arrived at the Abbey, he rode into the stables to leave his horse with a groom.

Then he entered the house, not by the main entrance but by a side-door, and found his way without much difficulty to the first floor.

He met a housemaid, who looked surprised to see him, but dropped him a respectful curtsy as he said:

"I want to speak to Lady Caroline."

"I thinks Her Ladyship'll be in her Sitting-Room, Your Grace. Shall I tell Her Ladyship Your Grace wishes to see her?"

"No, just show me the way," the Duke ordered.

The maid took him up the staircase to the second floor, and without waiting to be announced, he opened the door.

Caroline was sitting on a sofa and beside her was Edward Dalkirk.

They were talking earnestly and holding each other's hands as the Duke entered. They looked up with astonishment, then rose somewhat guiltily to their feet.

"I am sorry to interrupt you, Caroline," the Duke said, "but I wish to see you privately without your mother and father knowing I have come to the Abbey."

"I will go . . . ." Edward Dalkirk began, but the Duke held out his hand.

"I am glad to see you again, Dalkirk," he said. "I was in fact coming over to see you in the near future, but this will save me from doing so."

Edward Dalkirk, who was a good-looking young man with honest eyes, looked surprised and the Duke went on:

"Elfa has told me you have a number of good mares. I thought perhaps you would like to use my stallions, which I can say without conceit are outstanding."

For a moment Edward Dalkirk was speechless.

"Use your—stallions—Your Grace?" he said at length.

"It seems foolish not to do so when we are such near neighbours," the Duke said, "but perhaps it would be even better if we went into partnership."

It seemed as if Edward Dalkirk were too stunned to reply, but Caroline gave a little cry.

"Do you mean . . . that? Do you . . . really mean it?" she asked. "If Edward were in partnership with you, then I am sure Papa would . . . allow us to be married."

"That was what I thought," the Duke smiled.

"I cannot . . . believe it!" Caroline exclaimed.

"I do not know what to say, Your Grace . . ." Edward began.

"I do not want you to say anything," the Duke interrupted, "but go and see the Head Groom in charge of my stables, and arrange everything between you."

As Edward Dalkirk tried to stammer his thanks, the Duke turned to Caroline.

"There is something I want to ask you," he said.

"Yes, of course," she replied.

Edward Dalkirk, still trying to find words in which to express his feelings, turned towards the door.

"Wait!" Caroline cried. "But do not let anybody see you!"

He smiled to show he understood her instructions and shut the door behind him.

Caroline looked at the Duke.

"How can I thank you . . ." she began.

"You can do that by telling me where you think Elfa has gone," the Duke said.

He saw Caroline's eyes widen and added quickly:

"No, we have not quarrelled. We are happy—as happy as you and Dalkirk will be—but several unwanted guests arrived and she has wisely hidden herself until they have left."

Caroline looked bewildered and the Duke said:

"I have learnt that she left early this morning on Swallow, and I do not think she would go far."

"No, I am sure she would not do that."

"Then where would she go?" the Duke persisted. "Has she any great friend in the neighbourhood?"

Caroline thought for a moment; then she made a sound that was almost a cry.

"Of course! I know where she would have gone," she said. "To her old Governess, Miss Mathieson. She went there once before when Papa had upset her."

"Where does Miss Mathieson live?"

"About ten miles away, on the very southern end of Papa's Estate in the village of Little Welham."

"I feel sure I know it," the Duke murmured.

"That is where she will be," Caroline said reassuringly. "At Honeysuckle Cottage."

"Thank you," the Duke said, "and please do not tell your parents what I have asked you, and I hope they will not be aware that I have called."

"Papa has gone to a meeting," Caroline replied, "and Mama is in her garden, so you are quite safe."

When she tried to thank the Duke again, he did not wait to hear her. Instead he hurried down the staircase back to the stables and a few minutes later was on his way home.

Back at Chester House, he realised with a sense of relief that it was still too early for Isobel or Kitty to be about, but he also had no wish to encounter George Hampton or Edward Fenwick.

He therefore went up to his bedroom to change from his riding-clothes and sent his valet to ask Harry Sheldon to come to him.

Harry arrived quickly.

"What are you up to, Silvanus?" he asked. "You did not breakfast with us, and when I asked just now, I was told you had gone riding."

"Now listen to me," the Duke said. "I am leaving, and you told me once that you would pay back the debt you owed me by helping me when I needed it."

"What are you asking me to do?" Harry asked suspiciously.

"I want you to get rid of Isobel once and for all," the Duke said, "and look after the house while I am away."

His friend stared at him in stupefaction.

"What are you saying?" he asked.

"It is not difficult," the Duke said, tying his tie expertly. "You will be in a position of authority until I return and, most important of all, needless to say, is for you to keep an eye on the horses."

"Where are you going? When will you be back?" Harry asked.

"Quite frankly, I cannot answer your last question, as I have no idea, and where I am going is a secret between Elfa and me."

Harry looked at him. Then he said slowly:

"I have the idea, and I do not think I am wrong, Silvanus, that you have fallen in love!"

"I am happy for the first time in my life," the Duke answered.

"I am delighted, but I am not particularly pleased at having to clear up the debris!"

"There is nobody else I can trust," the Duke replied simply.

Harry made a grimace as he said:

"You must be aware how Isobel will behave."

"Make it clear I have no wish to see her again," the Duke said, "and I think Kitty, who has quite a lot of common sense, will support you in agreeing that her behaviour last night was inexcusable."

"And if she refuses to go? What shall I do then?" Harry asked.

"Throw her out, or better still, let her become bored with the country. She will soon find it insufferably dull . . . ."

"Without you!" Harry finished.

"Exactly!" the Duke agreed.

He put on a smart whip-cord coat; then he turned to smile at his friend and held out his hand.

"Thank you, Harry, and everything in the house is at your disposal."

"For how long?" Harry enquired.

"Until Elfa and I are ready to return to civilisation."

Looking at him, Harry was thinking that could be a long time. He had never seen the Duke look so happy or so carefree.

There was also something in his expression which made Harry feel he had been through an experience which had changed him in a manner which he could not put into words.

It was not that it had made him grow older, but somehow bigger in himself and his character. Harry had a deep affection for the Duke, and he knew it was everything he had wanted for him, and yet up to now, it was something he had missed.

"Give my love to Elfa," he said. "I knew when I first saw her she was different, not only in looks but in character, from any woman I have ever met."

He thought there was a sudden light in the Duke's eyes and he went on:

"I am not being clairvoyant, Silvanus, when I say that this time you will not be disillusioned or bored."

"That is what I am sure of myself," the Duke replied simply. "Come and see me off."

They went to a side-door where the Duke had ordered his horses to be waiting for him.

Harry understood that he had no wish to say good-bye to anybody else or be forced to make explanations as to the reason for his precipitate departure.

The Travelling Chaise that was waiting for the Duke was the fastest vehicle he owned, and the team of chestnuts pulling it were, as Harry knew, the most outstanding horses in his stable.

What surprised him was that there were two out-riders, also on extremely well-bred horses. Harry real-ised that the Duke was intending to travel a long way, but he was careful enough to make no comment.

"Thank you, Harry!" the Duke said as he stepped into the Chaise and took the reins from a groom, who jumped up into the seat behind.

Then as the Duke drove off, Harry realised it was with an eagerness that he could not conceal.

He drove to the village of Little Welham without difficulty, and found Honeysuckle Cottage on the outskirts, which, as he had anticipated, had a wood behind it.

The Duke jumped down without waiting for his groom to knock on the door, and when it was opened, he found himself confronted by an elderly, white-haired woman who looked exactly like a retired Gov-erness.

"You must be Miss Mathieson," the Duke said.

The elderly woman smiled and bobbed him a curtsy as she replied:

"And I am sure you are His Grace the Duke of Lynchester. Elfa thought you might follow her, but you are here sooner than she expected."

"Where is she?" the Duke asked, as if he could not wait.

"You will find her, Your Grace, in the wood. She

told me she had something to think about and went there almost as soon as she arrived."

The Duke did not wait for the end of the explanation.

He walked past Miss Mathieson and out to the other side of the cottage through a back-door.

There was a small, well-kept garden, and at the end of it a wooden gate which led him directly into the wood.

There was a path winding among the miscellaneous collection of beech and oak trees, and the Duke followed it until he saw, leaning against the trunk of a large tree, the person he sought.

Elfa was still wearing the skirt of the green silk habit in which she must have ridden away from Chester House, but she had taken off her jacket and her hat.

Her thin muslin blouse was a spot of light against the tree, and her hair as gold as if she had brought the sunshine down from the sky into the shadows of the wood.

The Duke stood still, looking at her. Then, as if she sensed his presence, she turned round and saw him.

For a moment her eyes widened; then she gave a cry of sheer joy and ran to him with her arms outstretched. He held her against him and kissed her until the wood seemed to swim dizzily round them.

Their hearts were beating frantically, and when the Duke raised his head the breath was coming quickly from between his lips.

"Silvanus! You are here!" Elfa murmured. "I did not think you would . . . find me so . . . quickly."

"How could you go away?" the Duke asked. "You were right to leave, my darling, although I wish you had waited and let me come with you."

"I did not think you would want to do that," Elfa replied.

"But I do," he said, "and now, because we have a long way to go, we must leave at once."

142

She looked at him questioningly and he said:

"It is a secret."

She gave a little laugh and slipped her hand into his.

"Then it will be very exciting because I am with you."

"As I want to be with you."

He started to walk with her along the path by which he had come until, as if he could not help himself, he stopped to kiss her once again, passionately, insistently and at the same time tenderly because she was so precious.

* * *

As the Duke had said, they had a long way to go and it was only late in the afternoon that Elfa saw the sea in the distance and felt the salt in the air.

Instinctively, because she guessed now where they were going, she moved a little closer to the Duke and knew she was not in the least tired, but because she was beside him, she was exhilarated with a joy that she had never known before.

As if the Duke understood, he just smiled at her and thought that the whole day had been as golden as sunshine. They were both so happy that they had not noticed the heat of the sun.

A few minutes later they drove into a small fishing village where there was a natural harbour, in which the Duke had moored his new yacht.

He had christened her the *Mermaid* and had her brought from the shipbuilders to the South Coast, where he owned some land. He had in fact been planning to use her a month or so later.

Now it was exactly what he wanted at this particular moment, and he thought that fate itself, or perhaps the gods with whom Elfa identified him, were taking a hand in their affairs and offering them an ideal honeymoon.

Before he had ridden over to the Towers this morning, he had sent a groom riding across country with his instructions, and as they drove down to the quay, he noted with satisfaction that the brake carrying Elfa's luggage, drawn by six horses which he had also ordered to leave home, had arrived.

She, however, had eyes only for the yacht and she realised that it had beautiful lines, besides being very much larger than she had ever expected a private vessel to be.

The Duke lifted her down from the Chaise, and though she was longing to step up the gang-plank and go aboard, she paused to pat the horses that had carried them so swiftly and to say good-bye to the groom.

"Make sure you give them a good rest before you return, Jim," the Duke ordered.

"Oi'll do that, Y'Grace."

"I thought they were like the horses that Apollo drives across the sky with his chariot of light," Elfa said.

The Duke's eyes twinkled.

"I actually borrowed them from him for this very special occasion!"

She laughed.

She knew as they turned to go aboard she had never met another man who would enter into her fantasies and not laugh at her for having them.

The yacht was, as might have been expected, exquisitely planned by the Duke and, with many technical innovations, it had a perfection which its Captain was certain would arouse the envy of every other private owner.

The Saloon was decorated in green, with green curtains over the port-holes and green sofas and chairs. The Duke thought that he must have known when he chose the colour that it was essentially Elfa's.

When they went below and he showed her the

Master Cabin, it was hard to believe once again that she had not stepped into a world of her dreams.

Not only were the walls a very pale jade, but in the centre there was a huge bed made of oak. The posts were carved to represent tree trunks, and on them, as well as on the canopy above, were carved all the woodland animals and birds—squirrels, rabbits, stoats, pigeons, woodpeckers, jays, magpies and owls.

It was so skillfully done, with each carving so life-like, that Elfa looked to the Duke for an explanation.

"When I was building the yacht," he said, "I found an old craftsman in a village on my estate who showed me some of his work, and I ordered him to make this bed. You will be the *first* person to sleep in it, my darling, just as you are the *first* guest who has ever come aboard the *Mermaid*."

Elfa knew from the way he spoke that his words had a special meaning for her, as he remembered what she had said to him after he had kissed her at Devonshire House.

She could not, however, help recalling the Count-ess's words about going to Paris, and she asked, with just a little note of apprehension in the tone of her voice:

"Where . . . are we . . . going?"

The Duke put his arms around her as he said:

"We will go anywhere in the world you like, my adorable one, but I thought we would start by sailing along the coast of England to Cornwall, where I have a house I have not visited for many years, and never since I was a man."

Elfa knew he was telling her that he had never been there with another woman, and he went on:

"It belonged to my mother's family, and she left it to me when she died. It stands near the sea and is surrounded by trees which grow right down to the beach, and we can be alone. Nobody shall interrupt us."

145

Elfa gave a little sigh of sheer happiness.

"It sounds too perfect, too wonderful!" she murmured. "I am so happy that I am ... afraid."

"Afraid?" he asked.

"The gods might be jealous."

"I will protect you even from the gods," the Duke said.

He pulled her still closer to him and turned her face up to his.

"How can I have found anybody so perfect? So exquisite, so unique?" he asked.

She smiled at him and he said fiercely:

"You are mine and I will never, never share you with anybody! I am already insanely jealous not only of other people, but of anything that holds your interest or even your thoughts."

"There is no ... reason for you to be ... jealous," Elfa replied. "You know as well as I do that I am yours ... completely and absolutely yours."

Her voice was very soft as she went on:

"Last night ... when you loved me ... I knew that I had no identity apart from you ... and we are one person as closely, as completely ... as if we were enclosed in the trunk of a tree."

She knew the Duke was listening and she went on:

"But a tree has branches and leaves and gives people shade and protection .... that is what you already do, and perhaps ... I can help you a little ... with your responsibilities to others."

The Duke found it hard for a moment to reply.

He knew that all the women in whom he had been interested and who had certainly given him their hearts had never given a thought to what he did for anyone else.

He also knew, as he had known this morning, that Elfa was opening up new horizons for him, giving him new ideals and new objectives in life.

"I understand what you are saying to me, my

precious darling," he said, "and I shall try not to disappoint you, but for the moment, before we do anything else, I am entitled to a honeymoon."

Elfa's eyes were shining as she said:

"I thought when I saw the *Mermaid* that that was what you intended."

"She will carry us away into a dream-world," the Duke said, "where we can tell each other of our love until you decide, and it will be your decision only, that we should return and take up the burdens that will be waiting for us."

Elfa smiled at him.

"They will not be burdens," she said, "because we will be together, and, darling Silvanus, however much you may have to do, there will always be ... special times when we can be ... alone."

Without meaning to, she glanced at the huge carved bed as she spoke, and the Duke gave a laugh that was a very happy sound.

"You may be quite sure of that, my enchanting Elf," he said. "The busiest man at least has his nights of moonlight, stars, dreams, and of course—love."

His voice deepened. Then he said:

"I am going now to order dinner to be ready as soon as you are. We have had a long day, my darling, and I think we should go to bed early."

Elfa did not answer. She merely lifted her lips to his.

He kissed her passionately, demandingly, and knew as he did so that this was only the beginning, and he not only had so much to teach her, but so much to learn himself.

To do so would not only be the most exciting, thrilling thing he had ever imagined, but also a new experience he had never expected to find.

* * *

The Duke accepted a glass of brandy, and when it had been poured out, the stewards left the Saloon.

He lifted his glass.

"To you, my adorable wife!" he said, "and to a honeymoon which, whatever else happens, we will repeat every year so that we shall never forget this, our first voyage together."

Elfa lifted her own glass.

"To Silvanus!" she said softly.

There was no need for her to add any adjectives or endearments. The way she spoke, the love in her eyes and the soft curve of her lips told the Duke what she was feeling.

As her evening-gown was the same colour as the walls of the Saloon, she looked as if she came from the sea and belonged to the sea, even though he knew he would always connect her with the woods.

As they ate an excellent meal cooked by an exceptionally fine Chef, he thought that every word they spoke to each other seemed to stimulate his mind. He found himself thinking thoughts which had never entered his head before and having new ideas which came to him as if they were an inspiration from some higher power.

"What are you thinking?" Elfa asked.

"I am feeling as if I could climb the highest mountain, rule the world in a new and enlightened fashion and join the gods on Olympus, who might be embarrassed by my superiority."

"That is where you belong," Elfa said. "At the same time I think the gods realise that their real mission is to help mankind. Through them the Greeks brought light to the world and set people thinking in a way different from before."

"That is what you have done to me," the Duke said.

"I want to believe that," Elfa remarked, "but I expect you would have found it for yourself, except that love is a great stimulant."

"I thought young girls knew nothing about love," the Duke teased.

"Not earthly love," Elfa replied. "The love you ... gave me is different from what I ... expected or what I ... imagined. Yet at the same time there was a familiarity about it because it was the love I listened to in the woods, the love I felt coming to me from the trees, and the love I reached for in my dreams."

"We will dream together," the Duke said firmly.

As he spoke he put his hand across the table; when she placed hers in it, he raised it to his lips.

The yacht had been moving on a smooth sea with a faint wind behind her ever since they had left the small harbour.

Now Elfa heard the anchor being let down and looked to the Duke for an explanation.

"We are stopping in a bay for the night," he told her. "It not only gives the crew a chance to rest, but prevents us from being disturbed. That is why I think now, my precious bride, it is time for us to go below."

Elfa saw the fire in his eyes as he spoke, and the colour rose in her cheeks.

The Duke rose and, drawing her to her feet, put his arms around her as they went down the companionway.

They walked along the passage which led to the Master Suite, and when they went into it Elfa saw that the Duke's valet had laid out her nightgown and turned down the bed, but there was no servant there.

"I am ... afraid you will have to ... undo my gown," she said to the Duke.

"I have every intention of doing so," he replied. "When we reach my house in Cornwall, there will be housemaids to attend to you, but here in the *Mermaid* I will wait on you, my lovely one, and I shall find it very exciting."

"You make me feel ... shy," Elfa protested.

"You were not shy last night," the Duke said.

"That was different," she replied. "Then you were Silvanus the ... god I have always worshipped but ... tonight you are ... a man."

149

She spoke the last word very softly, and the Duke said:

"A man who adores and worships you, a man who knows that if he is a god you are his goddess. But you are also, my darling, a woman."

He held her against him, and as her head fell back against his shoulder he looked down at her strange, elfin face.

He ran his finger over her little arched eyebrows, touched her eyes and her small, straight nose. Then he outlined the curve of her lips.

As he did so he felt her quiver with a sensuous movement that was very human, and he laughed gently.

"I can excite you, my adorable Elf!" he said, "and I am glad I can do so, for you excite me to madness!"

"I want ... to ... excite you," Elfa said, and the words came breathlessly from between her lips.

"You not only excite me," the Duke said, "but you bewitch and enslave me."

His hand slipped down her neck to the softness of her breast, as he went on:

"And that is not all: I am enchanted, my adorable one, not only by your face and your body, but by your spirit, your heart and your soul, and it is an enchantment from which I can never escape."

Elfa's gown fell to the floor and he lifted her into the strangely carved bed. For a moment she felt as if she were in the woods by the magic pool.

Then she knew it did not matter where she was as long as the Duke was there with her. As he joined her she put out her arms, pulling him close, feeling the strength and hardness of his body against hers.

"I love ... you," she whispered.

"I want you," the Duke said, "I want you completely and absolutely, now and for eternity."

His lips were fierce and she felt the fire on them, but she was neither shy nor afraid. This was the power of love omnipotent and godlike.

She surrendered herself to him, melting against him, feeling the beat of his heart on hers, his mouth holding her captive.

Then there was only love and the soft lap of the sea.

ABOUT THE AUTHOR

BARBARA CARTLAND, the world's most famous romantic novelist, who is also an historian, playwright, lecturer, political speaker and television personality, has now written over 300 books.

She has also had many historical works published and has written four autobiographies as well as the biographies of her mother and that of her brother Ronald Cartland, who was the first Member of Parliament to be killed in W.W. II. This book has a preface by Sir Winston Churchill and has just been republished with an introduction by Sir Arthur Bryant.

Barbara Cartland has sold 200 million books over the world, more than half of these in the U.S.A. She broke the world record in 1975 by writing twenty-three books and the four subsequent years with 20, 21, 23 and 24. In addition her album of love songs has just been published, sung with the Royal Philharmonic Orchestra.

Barbara Cartland, who is a Dame of the Order of St. John of Jerusalem has championed the cause for old people and founded the first Romany Gypsy Camp in the world.

Barbara Cartland is deeply interested in Vitamin Therapy and is President of the British National Association for Health. Her book the *Magic of Honey* has sold in millions all over the world.

She has a magazine *The World of Romance* and her Barbara Cartland Romantic World Tours will, in conjunction with British Airways, carry travelers to England, Egypt, India, France, Germany and Turkey.

Barbara Cartland

The world's bestselling author of romantic fiction. Her stories are always captivating tales of intrigue, adventure and love.

☐	13830	THE DAWN OF LOVE	$1.75
☐	14504	THE KISS OF LIFE	$1.75
☐	14503	THE LIONESS AND THE LILY	$1.75
☐	13942	LUCIFER AND THE ANGEL	$1.75
☐	14084	OLA AND THE SEA WOLF	$1.75
☐	14133	THE PRUDE AND THE PRODIGAL	$1.75
☐	13032	PRIDE AND THE POOR PRINCESS	$1.75
☐	13984	LOVE FOR SALE	$1.75
☐	14248	THE GODDESS AND THE GAIETY GIRL	$1.75
☐	14360	SIGNPOST TO LOVE	$1.75
☐	14361	FROM HELL TO HEAVEN	$1.75
☐	14585	LOVE IN THE MOON	$1.95
☐	14650	DOLLARS FOR THE DUKE	$1.95
☐	14791	A NIGHT OF GAIETY	$1.95
☐	14750	DREAMS DO COME TRUE	$1.95
☐	20301	ENCHANTED	$1.95

Buy them at your local bookstore or use this handy coupon:

Bantam Books, Inc., Dept. BC2, 414 East Golf Road, Des Plaines, Ill. 60016

Please send me the books I have checked above. I am enclosing $_____ (please add $1.00 to cover postage and handling). Send check or money order —no cash or C.O.D.'s please.

Mr/Mrs/Miss_____

Address_____

City_____State/Zip_____

BC2—8/81

Please allow four to six weeks for delivery. This offer expires 2/82.